Search for Last Chance

Other Five Star Titles
by A. L. McWilliams:

Eye of the Cat
Penny Town Justice

Search for Last Chance

A. L. McWilliams

Five Star • Waterville, Maine

This novel is a work of fiction. Names, characters, places and incidents are either the product of the author's imagination, or, if real, used fictitiously.

Five Star First Edition Romance Series.

Published in 2001 in conjunction with
The Seymour Agency.

Set in 11 pt. Plantin by Myrna S. Raven.

Printed in the United States on permanent paper.

Library of Congress Cataloging-in-Publication Data

McWilliams, A. L. (Audra LaVaun)
    Search for last chance / A. L. McWilliams.
        p. cm.—(Five Star first edition romance series)
    ISBN 0-7862-3697-3 (hc : alk. paper)
    1. Treasure-trove—Fiction. I. Title. II. Series.
PS3563.C927 S43 2001
813´.6—dc21   2001040879

To Linda McWilliams and Oscar Pereida.

I love you both.

CHAPTER ONE

Lucky, Texas: August, 1888

Jesse Watts paused just inside the open doorway of the Deputy U.S. Marshal's office and waited for his eyes to adjust to the gloom. The room before him was small, hot, and dusty, and stank of bad breath and unwashed bodies.

"You're the marshal?" he asked.

The greasy mound of flesh seated behind the desk stirred, raised sleepy eyes to look at him, and nodded.

Stepping forward, Jesse produced a sweat-dampened piece of paper from his right hip pocket. He unfolded it carefully so as not to tear it and handed it to the marshal. It was a reward dodger bearing the name, sketchy description, and nefarious deeds of an outlaw worth nine hundred dollars to Wells, Fargo & Company. "I was told in Amarillo there's a man lives around here who resembles this description," he said. "Maybe you know where I can find him."

Marshal Young read the handbill slowly, taking one word at a time, brow furrowed in concentration. Finished, he shrugged indifferently. "You a bounty hunter or something?"

One corner of Jesse's mouth lifted in what passed for a smile. "I'm a manhunter," he said and gestured to the limp piece of paper. "Have you seen him?"

Again, the marshal shrugged, yawned, and scratched his head. "Maybe. Maybe not." He examined the scurf beneath his fingernails. "Memory ain't so good anymore."

Jesse scowled, knowing what was coming. He watched Marshal Young stare at the handbill, saw the frown on his face deepen as he tried hard to remember, really putting an effort into it. He missed his calling, Jesse thought. He should've been an actor. "Shell Paxton." The marshal mouthed the name softly and squinted one eye in thought. "Sounds mighty familiar."

Tired of the performance, Jesse lifted the barrel of his Winchester repeater which, until now, had been resting in the bend of his left arm.

"This should jog your memory."

Marshal Young never batted an eye. He mopped the sweat from his face and scratched his armpits. "A share of that nine-hunnerd-dollar bounty might do better," he suggested.

"Mister, you shouldn't have said that."

Jesse jacked a shell into the Winchester's chamber and squeezed the trigger.

The report exploded off the walls of the tiny room, and the marshal dove out of sight behind his desk. Gunsmoke curled from the muzzle of Jesse's rifle.

He waited. Several seconds passed before he heard a grunt and saw Young slowly rise. The marshal glanced at him, then looked at the small, jagged hole in the wall behind him and a scant two inches above where his head had been. The walls were thin, and a skinny beam of sunlight slanted through the bullet hole.

"Shell Paxton lives somewhere around here," Jesse said in a quiet voice. "I'm not familiar with this country, so you're gonna take me to him."

Marshal Young nodded in agreement and picked up his hat. "Be glad to."

On a map, Lucky, Texas, was marked by a single, insignificant dot in the middle of nowhere, and in reality the town was even less noteworthy than its symbol. It was a dying, dust-blown fragment of hell populated by a handful of drunks and three or four starving mutts, and the disturbance in the marshal's office didn't receive much attention from either party. Even the existence of a Deputy U.S. Marshal in Lucky would soon be a thing of the past, for his headquarters were scheduled to be moved to nearby Amarillo.

In the time it took Marshal Young to round up a team and buckboard, Jesse Watts tightened the cinch on his horse and smoked three cigarettes down to their butts. He was working on the fourth when the buckboard swung onto the town's single street. It was a rattling, bone-jarring contraption, and each revolution of the left front wheel brought forth a piercing squeak.

Fat cheeks jiggling, Marshal Young sawed on the reins and pulled up in front of Jesse. "Ready to go?"

Short on patience, long on temper, Jesse growled an obscenity under his breath as he stepped into the saddle and swung his horse alongside the buckboard, and the two men left the little town of Lucky behind them. A hot, dry wind was blowing out of the south, taking the topsoil and half a million tumbleweeds with it, and Jesse tightened the chin strap on his hat to keep it from joining the migration. The wind in this country was sleepless, so one either learned to live with it or left, because there was nothing in the flat, treeless land to stop it.

Marshal Young glanced over at him. "You might as well know something!" He had to shout above the racket of the buckboard. "He goes by the name of Shell Warner, not Paxton!"

Jesse frowned. "But you knew who he was?"

"I was pretty sure!"

"Then why in the hell didn't you arrest him?"

"Around here," Young said, "folks generally mind their

own business. So long as Shell didn't bother nobody, I left him alone."

"Until you saw how much he was worth," Jesse remarked dryly. "How far from town does he live?"

Young thought a moment. "It's about an hour's ride."

"What does he do? Farm or ranch?"

"Used to do both. Drouth wiped him out, though. He works for the Anchor Land and Cattle Company now."

"Doing what?"

"Greasing windmills, digging post holes, stretching bobwire . . . jobs the straight riding hands won't touch," he replied. "Him and his wife live at the edge of the Anchor holdings. Been living there nigh onto five years now, but the land ain't his no more."

Jesse was surprised. A man on the run from the law had no business getting married. Though if Shell Paxton had been living out here five years, he was hardly running. He had simply withdrawn from the public eye. Jesse had been hunting him for about a year, and he understood now why it had taken so long to track him down. A man who stays in one place leaves no sign. According to the reward dodger, he was wanted in California for numerous train and stagecoach robberies, all of them performed in the company of Vic Taylor and three or more other unidentified outlaws. While Taylor was the gang's apparent leader, Shell Paxton was second-in-command. Agents of Wells, Fargo & Company hoped that the arrest and interrogation of Paxton would help them locate his partner. Jesse hoped so, too, for old Vic Taylor was worth an impressive three thousand dollars, dead or alive, and Jesse expected to collect every cent of it.

Bounty hunting for Jesse Watts was a hobby as well as a trade. He enjoyed his work and was good at it, the best in the business. He had started in a small way, bagging coyotes, wolves, and mountain lions for the rewards put up by ranchers before moving on to larger game, the two-legged variety. His reputation as a bloodhound and exterminator had quickly spread throughout the western states and territories. It was a distinction he was proud of and intended to maintain.

While Jesse Watts' methods of tracking down killers and thieves sometimes bordered on being crimes in themselves, the law generally gave him a wide berth. The important result was that, one way or another, he always got the job done.

"What's Paxton like?" he asked suddenly, wanting to know more about the man before he actually confronted him.

Marshal Young shrugged. "Shell keeps to himself mostly. Never has much to say, but he's friendly enough if you can ever get him to talking. He's never caused me any trouble." Pausing, he looked at Jesse and grinned. "His wife used to work in some fancy hurdy gurdy out in Colorado."

"A soiled dove, eh? Have any kids?"

"Any what?"

"Kids!"

Young shook his head, blew his nose, and crammed the wadded up handkerchief back into his pocket. "They lost both their young'uns. Scarlet fever took their little girl last spring."

The squeaking of the buckboard's left front wheel was gradually becoming more pronounced, causing the horses to lay back their ears and kick the dashboard in protest, and tired of shouting over the racket, the two men fell silent.

Jesse studied the bleak terrain. Several times, he had seen scatterings of bones—hollow-eyed skulls with long, crooked horns, a few disconnected vertebrae, leg bones, ribs—all that remained of some poor cowman's assets. Whether it was the fierce blizzards of 1886 that had killed them or this summer's drouth, Jesse didn't know, but they certainly hadn't died from overeating. The only sign of life in all this wide-open country was the tired, late summer green of an occasional mesquite tree. The sun had long since sapped everything else dry, leaving behind a drab mixture of grays, yellows, and browns.

Presently, they came to a barbed wire fence, and Marshal Young stopped the team. Four strands of bright, new wire stretched before them, blocking what had once been a well-traveled wagon road. Young gave the fence and its owners a sound cussing, then turned to Jesse.

"Texas passed a law making it a felony to cut a fence down, but I'm almighty tempted to break it."

"Looks like they started a new road," Jesse said, and he pointed out a dim trail that broke off from the main one to follow the fenceline. "Maybe it'll lead us to a gate."

They headed out again, and after a mile or so, found the gate Jesse had predicted. Dismounting, he opened it and crossed over the boundary onto range owned by the Anchor.

As it turned out, the new route was the shorter of the two and passed close to Shell Paxton's house. Jesse could see a couple of small, weathered buildings in the distance and nearby these was a dry creek bed that probably hadn't been dry when Paxton settled here five years ago. The early '80s had been unusually wet years for this part of the country. Jesse figured that Paxton and his wife, like so many other families, had staked out their claim, put in their first crops, and likely had some success in those early years. Then came the long drouths and failed crops, and to keep from starving, Paxton had sold his land to the rancher he now worked for, too poor to stay, too poor to leave. It was a tight fix for any man to be in, and Jesse guessed he'd be doing him a favor by taking him back to California.

Alert now, he rode ahead of the marshal with his rifle

laying across his lap. He loosened the revolver in his waistband. Down by the creek, hidden among the brush, a cow bawled to her calf, and cicadas buzzed the afternoon away. Jesse slowed his mount to a walk as he rode into the yard and looked around him. There was a pleasant, peaceful aura about the Paxtons' home that surprised him. Weathered a silvery gray, the house was small but soundly built, and curtains of a pretty calico covered the windows. A short walk made of flat, gray stones led to the door. Behind the house were a barn and mesquite-pole corral where a couple of horses dozed in the sunshine and swished flies from each other's faces with their tails.

Listening to the chickens cackling and clucking in the yard, Jesse dismounted in front of the house and glanced over his shoulder at Marshal Young as he stopped the team a short distance behind him.

"Reckon he's home?"

Young nodded. "It's Sunday. And his horse is here."

"Good. You keep an eye out, make sure he doesn't slip out the back way."

Rifle resting in the bend of his arm, Jesse walked up to the door and was about to knock when it suddenly opened and a young woman in a faded cotton dress looked out at him.

She was small, a scant inch or two over five feet, and the most pleasing sight Jesse had seen since his arrival in Texas. Several strands of auburn hair had come loose from the chignon in back of her head, and she brushed them aside and left a black streak across her forehead. Jesse noticed then that her hands were stained with stove blacking.

She appeared out of sorts and didn't waste any time with formalities. "What d'you want?"

Before Jesse could open his mouth, Marshal Young spoke up from his perch on the buckboard seat. "Sally, this here's

Mr. Watts. He wants a word with Shell."

Jesse saw caution enter the woman's blue eyes, as if she already suspected why he was here.

"Ma'am," he said, "it's pretty hot standing out in the sun like this. What do you say we go inside?"

"You'll have to come back some other time," she said. "Shell ain't here."

"Now, Sally . . ." Marshal Young clucked like an old fat hen and shook his head. "You trot inside and tell him he's got company."

Sally Paxton frowned at the marshal, and when she spoke again, her manner was even less friendly than before. "Shell's taking a nap. Y'all best just go on back to town."

She retreated as if to close the door, but Jesse was ready for it. He stuck out his foot and grasped the door, pushing it open, and was about to force his way inside when a man walked up behind Sally, moved past her, and blocked the doorway.

Stripped to the waist, barefoot, unarmed, Shell Paxton fastened the top button on his denims and barely stifled a yawn. There was a red crease pressed into the side of his face from a wrinkle in the pillow.

Squinting in the bright sunlight, he looked past Jesse at Marshal Young. "What's the problem, Harry?"

"I'm afraid you are," Jesse broke in, and he tipped the barrel of his rifle up so that it was aimed at the young man's stomach. "One wrong move, Paxton, and I'll blast you clean out the back door."

He heard the woman gasp, saw her clutch her husband's arm, nails digging deeply into his flesh. Shell Paxton's face clouded. He started to back away from the door, then seemed to think better of it.

Jesse motioned him outside. "Turn and face the wall and

keep those hands up where I can see 'em."

Keeping a wary eye on the rifle, Paxton did as he was ordered, and Jesse stepped aside to allow Marshal Young the honor of cuffing the outlaw's hands.

He hadn't expected to take Paxton without a fight. It was almost disappointing, and he studied his prisoner critically. Shell Paxton wasn't much taller than his wife. He was brown as a Mexican and built like a whipcord—strong and tightly knit—and hair that should have been dark was bleached a shade or two lighter by the sun.

His hands now cuffed behind his back, Paxton glanced at his wife's frightened face before turning calm eyes on Jesse. "Can I at least get some clothes on before you haul me into town?"

Jesse considered his request, rolled his tongue around inside his mouth, and finally nodded. "I reckon so." He nodded toward the girl. "Go get his shirt and boots."

"Thank you," Paxton said. "Who are you anyway?"

"Name's Jesse Watts. I've been hunting you for quite a spell."

Recognizing him, the young outlaw nodded. "Bounty hunter, huh?" He favored Jesse with a halfhearted smile. "You fellas just don't give up, do you?"

CHAPTER TWO

Feet crossed at the ankles, hands clasped behind his head, Shell Paxton lay on his back on a hard bunk and stared up at the low, dingy ceiling of his cell. Though the marshal's office and the jailhouse in Lucky were separate buildings, he could hear the muffled blast of Harry Young blowing his nose. It sounded like a foghorn.

Shell turned his head slightly to survey his new home. The jailhouse was a tiny, two-cell affair with poor lighting and practically no ventilation, and the smell oozing from the slop bucket in the corner of his cell was nauseating. A life-sized drawing of a voluptuous, nude woman decorated the far wall, a figment of some poor drunk's fantasies, and the artist's name was written in large letters across her left breast.

Shell gazed at the name, wondering idly what it said and wishing he hadn't put off letting Sally teach him to read. He had waited too long. Where had the time gone? Six years of work and worry and too few pleasures, yet the time had slipped past without his even realizing it. Now he had nothing, not even his freedom.

Thinking back on everything he and Sally had lost this past year, thinking about the round-faced, brown-eyed little girl who had been their daughter, and the fever that had literally burned the life out of her, a deep weariness overwhelmed Shell. He closed his eyes, wishing he could shut out the memory as well.

They had had such high hopes. After a year of marriage, the Paxtons had moved from Colorado to Shell's native Texas to build a home and a new life for themselves, and for a time, it looked as if they might beat the odds. For three years, they kept their heads above the ocean of red ink so many farmers and small ranchers were drowning in, and the satisfaction of owning his own land and livestock had seemed to Shell well worth the hard work and sacrifice. At the same time, Texas's sparsely settled High Plains offered him a measure of security from the law. For the first time in his life, he experienced a sense of peace and stability.

Shell opened his eyes and drew a deep breath. That's all gone now, he told himself, and there's nothing you can do to get it back, so don't think about it.

He thought instead about what lay ahead of him. Likely, Jesse Watts would keep him jailed here until an official from California picked him up. Then what? He would be tried for armed robbery, of course, and convicted and sentenced to spend a few years of his life in San Quentin, and Sally would live with her sister in St. Louis until he finished serving his time. It was a bleak outlook for them both.

The system was supposed to be just, but Shell could see little fairness in this. If a man reformed himself and wasn't bothering anyone, Shell figured he should be left alone. Save the prison space for someone who really deserved it.

But try telling that to a judge. Shell guessed if he had as much money and influence as Wells, Fargo & Company, people would damned well listen to him, but a poor man had about as much chance in a courtroom as a wax cat in hell.

Beyond the stone walls of the jailhouse, Shell could hear men's voices and the jingle of keys. It had been less than twenty-four hours since the bounty hunter appeared on his and Sally's doorstep, and already the whole county seemed to have learned of his arrest. While Sally hadn't been allowed to visit him, Marshal Young had let four or five of his friends come in and look at the scoundrel who had sided the infamous Vic Taylor in countless robberies. They had gawked at him, shaking their heads, unable to believe that a hardened criminal had been living under their noses for five years without their knowing it. For the first time in Lucky's history, the townsfolk had something to gossip about.

The jailhouse door swung open, flooding the cell with light, and Shell felt exposed and unprotected, with no place to hide.

He sat up slowly, swinging his legs over the side of the bunk, and squinted his eyes in the sudden bright light. The silhouetted figures of two men, one short and fat, the other one all legs and arms, appeared momentarily in the doorway. Then the shortest of the two men shut the door, and Shell saw it was Marshal Young. The second man was the bounty hunter.

Arms folded across his chest, the marshal leaned against the door and gazed at his prisoner with sleepy-eyed disinterest while Jesse Watts approached Shell's cell and looked in at him between the bars.

Watts appeared to be in his late forties, an unfriendly looking man with pale, deeply set eyes, and the face beneath the scruffy beard was bony, the cheeks hollow. He regarded Shell with grim satisfaction.

"Comfortable?"

A faint smile touched Shell's mouth and eyes. "Couldn't be better."

"Your wife's been asking me if she can see you."

"What'd you tell her?"

"I told her if you cooperated with me, I might let her come in."

Shell leaned forward, resting both elbows on his knees. He studied Watts curiously. "Cooperate? How?"

Without answering, Jesse Watts laid his sidearm on the

floor, well out of Shell's reach, turned to Marshal Young, and held out his hand for the key to the cell. Young tossed it to him, and he unlocked the door and stepped inside. Dragging a three-legged stool toward him with his foot, Watts straddled it and sat across from Shell.

He drew a folded paper from his pocket. With a flick of his wrist, he dropped it at Shell's feet. "Read that first."

Reaching down, Shell picked up the paper and shook it out. Across the top in bold writing was the figure for a fairly large sum of money, nine hundred dollars to be exact, and below this, he recognized his own name. There was more writing in small print beneath his name, and though he couldn't read what it said, he knew it was a wanted dodger.

He handed it back to Watts. "Never realized I was so popular."

"Vic Taylor's worth three thousand."

Shell whistled in surprise.

Watts nodded. "I know. It's a lot of money." He fixed Shell with a hard stare. "And I aim to get it one way or another. You'll help me."

Shell knew it was coming to this even before he heard the words. He watched Jesse Watts light his cigarette and noticed the deep-set eyes still staring at him over his cupped hands. Watts dropped the match on the floor, and blue smoke puffed from his mouth and curled up from the burning tip of his cigarette. The match's sharp odor reached Shell after a moment and stung his nostrils.

"You'll help me," Watts said again.

"Think so?"

"I know so." For the first time, the bounty hunter smiled, and his teeth were the color of toasted bread. "The law in California wants you taken alive," he said, "but they never said how much alive." He leaned closer to Shell. "Half alive maybe? What d'you think, Paxton?"

When Shell didn't answer, Watts drew back and sucked hard on his cigarette before continuing. "I haven't sent a wire to California yet, so I can keep you here till you rot if I want to. Or until you answer my questions."

Shell pointed to Marshal Young with his chin. "What about him? He's the law. Not you."

"There's a bullet hole in the back wall of his office that says differently."

Shell looked from the marshal's bored, sunburned face to Jesse Watts and frowned slightly as he soaked in the full import of that last statement. So what the man was saying was that he was above the law and could do whatever he wanted. That didn't surprise him. It was the way of most bounty hunters.

"I know a few things about you and Vic Taylor," Watts said slowly. "I know you were more than partners. He was like a father to you. He took you under his wing when you were just a kid, and you stuck with him until . . . What? Five years ago?"

"Six."

Watts nodded. "So you know more about the old robber than anyone."

Shell said nothing.

"How's he looking these days, Paxton? Still big enough to shade an elephant?"

"I wouldn't know."

"I think you do."

Shell studied the bounty hunter a moment and in a quiet voice, said, "Think what you want."

Making no comment, Watts ground out his half-smoked cigarette, rolled another, and lit up. Shell watched him closely, sensing his impatience and wondering how far he could push this without getting killed.

Watts took several quick puffs on his cigarette before speaking. "Twice in the past four years, James Hume, a detective working for Wells Fargo, trailed Taylor to Texas but lost him both times. He was coming here to see you, wasn't he?"

"If he was, he never made it."

This was not true, and Watts knew it. "Paxton, you're a liar," he said and scowled. "Let's stop beating around the bush. Taylor's changed his tactics. He moves around more than he used to. He's spread out, not just hitting trains and stages in California, but all over the West, wherever there's pay dirt. But I have a feeling he's still using the same hideouts, and you know where they are." Again, Watts leaned toward Shell. "If the information you provide helps me catch Taylor, there's a possibility you could get a lighter sentence."

"And if I don't rat on him, what then?"

"Then I guess you'd better get ready for a long stay in this bird cage."

Hooking the heel of a heavy work shoe on the edge of his cot, Shell's gaze roamed around the jail before settling back on Jesse Watts, and a slow smile spread over his face. "Room and board, and the county foots the bill," he mused. "I guess that beats digging post holes all day."

It was the wrong thing to say to a man of Jesse Watts' temperament, but suddenly Shell didn't care. He was tired of threats, tired of being told what to do, not just by this man, but by everyone. He'd had a bellyful of it.

Sitting motionless on his stool, the cigarette smoking between his fingers, Watts' face seemed to stiffen. "So that's how it's gonna be."

"I guess it is," Shell replied, and he was no longer smiling.

The bounty hunter's mouth formed a tight line between

the black mustache and beard, and his hand closed on the cigarette and ground it out against his palm. He spread his fingers then, letting crumbles of tobacco and paper scatter to the floor, and the next thing Shell knew, the man was on his feet and lunging at him.

Watts' first blow glanced off his left cheekbone as he turned his face to avoid it, and his head banged hard against the wall. Kicking out at him, Shell rolled over, hit the floor on his side, and was halfway to his feet when Watts' knee came up and smashed into his mouth and nose. Blood spurted as he fell back against the wall.

Jesse Watts dove into him, breaking through his guard and keeping him pinned to the wall with the bone-crushing force of both fists. Their bodies were close, so close Shell never got a chance to strike back or even cover himself, and unhampered, the bounty hunter swung again and again, making each driving blow of his fists count and grunting with the effort. Watts worked on his stomach a while, then his face, and only when Shell's knees started to buckle under him did he back off.

Breathing hard and fast through his mouth, big hands hanging at his sides, Watts watched Shell brace himself against the bunk while his blood made bright crimson polka dots on the floor.

Still standing by the door, Marshal Young looked from one man to the other and cleared his throat. "If you kill him, do you still get the bounty?"

"If that was the case," Watts muttered, "I would've already put the mute bastard out of his misery."

Whipping out his knife, the bounty hunter took one long stride forward, grasped a fistful of Shell's hair, and yanked his head back. Shell almost choked. He felt the cold, sharp point of Watts' knife gouge into his exposed throat, breaking the skin.

"We'll do this every day until your tongue loosens up. How does that sound, Paxton? Sound like fun?"

Swallowing hard, clearing his mouth of bloody saliva, Shell started to speak but found the effort too much. He stared at Watts instead, his dark eyes cold and void of expression.

Cursing, Watts released him, tucked his knife into its sheath, and backed out of the cell. The door clanged shut behind him.

He spoke to Young. "Don't give him anything to eat or drink until I say to."

"What about his wife? She'll be asking to see him."

Watts glanced over his shoulder at Shell. "We'll let her come in sometime tomorrow. Maybe when she sees his face, she'll talk some sense into him."

Marshal Young nodded and opened the door.

"Watts!"

Surprised, both men turned and looked at their prisoner. It was the first time either of them had heard Shell Paxton raise his voice.

Shell pushed away from the wall, stumbled forward, and caught himself against the bars of his cell.

"You're wasting your time, Watts."

The tall man shook his head. "You'll talk."

"If that's what you think," Shell said slowly, "then I hope you like this town . . . because you'll be here a while." White-knuckled hands gripped the bars. "I'll outlast you."

Jesse Watts studied him a long moment. There was something about this cool, soft-spoken man that had him wondering.

Perhaps he would, at that.

23

CHAPTER THREE

What would Vic Taylor do?

The question nagged at Shell off and on throughout the night.

He wouldn't have let Jesse Watts catch up with him in the first place, Shell thought disgustedly. That was simple enough.

But even Vic could have an off day.

Lying on his side on the hard, narrow bed, Shell watched the light in the barred window slowly grow brighter and brighter with the dawning of a new day and thought about the beating Watts had given him the previous afternoon. What would Vic have done in his position? Picturing it, Shell smiled. Vic Taylor was a bear of a man with enough strength in his hands to bend a horseshoe, and he was a born brawler. The blood on the cell floor would not have been his.

He would have thrashed Watts, spat in his face, and made his escape.

Escape.

Holding his breath and wincing slightly, Shell pushed himself up into a sitting position, eyes still fixed on the window in the cell across from him. Yesterday, he had looked this smelly stone dungeon over from top to bottom only to reach the conclusion that the Lucky jailhouse was built to last. What it lacked in size and appearance it more than made up for in construction.

His best chance for escape would be sometime during the train ride to California, but he didn't know if he could hold out that long, certainly not if Jesse Watts kept his promise of the day before.

Shell knew he was being foolish. Tell the man what he wants to know and be done with it, he thought. That's what anyone with a lick of sense would do. But it's not that simple, is it? It's not even like you're so hell bent on protecting Vic. No, this goes deeper than that.

It's the principle of the matter.

Shell shivered a little, still chilled by the cool night air that had settled within the stone walls. He felt bad, and each intake of breath was accompanied by a liquid rattle in his lungs, a holdover from a childhood sickness that he couldn't seem to shake. It was worse this morning than usual, and he wished for a cup of coffee to drink, or a shot of whiskey, anything to clear his throat and warm his insides. Breakfast would also have lifted his spirits.

But the time dragged by, and still no one came to check on him, and Shell's thoughts turned more and more to Sally. He wanted to see her, to hear her voice, to touch her—the only good thing in his life that was left, and he needed her more now than ever.

He had met Sally Day in a dancehall in Leadville, Colorado, six years ago where he had taken more than a passing interest in her, and she in him, and within three weeks they were pronounced man and wife and celebrating their union in Denver. It had been a turning point in both their lives, and a good excuse for Shell to go straight, and live honestly for a change. As newlyweds, they had made a handsome pair and they were a team, able to work better together than apart. Nothing had changed that.

Something bit Shell on the chest, jolting him back to the present, and he rubbed the spot through his shirt, wondering what was under there and afraid he already knew. He didn't bother to look. Lice, ticks, spiders, flies—what did it matter? There was no escaping them.

With nothing to do except brood and scratch at his own filth, Shell counted the bars of his cell again. There were forty in all, twenty-five on one side, fifteen on the other, but he counted them over and over just the same.

Counting things was almost an obsession with Shell and had been ever since he was a kid. At home, he knew how many rafters there were in the barn and had counted the mesquite poles of the horse corral. He knew the exact number of small, white flowers on the curtains hanging in the bedroom window.

Shell judged it was past noon when he heard the metallic click and snap of a key being inserted in the jail door. The sound brought him to his feet, and he perked up considerably when he saw the girlish figure of his wife outlined in the open doorway.

They met at the bars, and Sally stared up at him, startled by his bruised, blood-crusted face.

"Oh, God, Shell," she whispered, "what are they doing to you?"

His swollen lips formed a smile. "It's not as bad as it looks."

She reached out to touch his face, but he drew back, his gaze shifting to Marshal Young.

"Where's Watts?"

Watching them from the doorway, Young shrugged. "Don't worry. He'll be along."

Sally looked over her shoulder at him. "Can we have some privacy?"

"No."

"Why not?"

"Cause Watts said to keep an eye on you."

"What's the matter? You think I have a file hidden under my dress?"

Young pulled at his nose and smiled. "No, but I could check to make sure."

"Careful, Harry."

There was a quiet warning in Shell's voice, and though a wall of iron bars separated the two men, Marshal Young didn't push it. Yawning, scratching his belly, he relented.

"Better enjoy yourselves," he said and turned his back to them, his shoulder resting against the door facing. "This may be the last time Watts lets you see each other."

Sally looked back up at Shell. Their faces were close enough together that Shell could have easily counted the twenty-seven freckles on her nose had he wished to.

"How are you holding up?" she asked.

He nodded. "I'm all right."

"You should've cooperated with Jesse Watts. Vic can take care of himself."

"Well, you know me. I have to pick the hard way."

She smiled, leaned closer, and kissed him between the bars, then glanced over her shoulder again to make sure the marshal wasn't watching. When she turned back to Shell, her eyes were alive with excitement.

"I'm getting you out of here."

Shell frowned. "Sally, don't do anything stupid."

"I have a gun."

The whispered words sent an electric shock through Shell's body, and his hands tightened on her shoulders.

"Where?"

"Under my dress."

A mischievous smile lit up her face. Shell looked past her at Marshal Young. Suspecting nothing, his back was still turned to them.

Keeping a wary eye on him, Sally hiked up her skirt and just above her left knee was Shell's gunbelt, wrapped twice around her thigh and buckled in place. She gave him a quick look, the question in her eyes, and he nodded.

"Now," he whispered.

Sally was slipping the gun from its holster when Marshal Young turned and saw her.

"What the heck . . ."

Swiftly, not thinking of the possible outcome, Shell's hand swept down, and he jerked the six-shooter from Sally and thumbed back the hammer as he brought it to bear on the lawman. With his left arm outstretched between the bars, he looked down the gun barrel at Harry Young and saw the sleepy expression vanish from the man's eyes.

"Come on. Move away from the door."

Young hesitated.

Shell's face tensed. "Harry, I've never had to kill anyone in my life. Don't you be the first."

Looking from the Peacemaker Colt to Shell's dark, deadly earnest face, Marshal Young eased away from the open door and slowly lifted his hands above his head.

Shell nodded, relieved. "That's it. Now with your left hand, unbuckle your gunbelt and let it fall, then toss your keys to Sally."

Without a word, the marshal did as he was instructed, and looping the gunbelt over one shoulder, Sally tried the keys until she found the one that unlocked the cell door. It swung open, and Shell Paxton was a free man.

Marshal Young backed up a step. "Now, Shell," he said, "I've always been real good to you. I've never lifted a finger against you."

"That was real big of you, Harry."

Young nodded, looking from Shell to Sally. "So y'all can't

blame me for this. It's all Jesse Watts' doings. Not mine."

"Maybe so," Shell said, "but I still can't trust you."

Marshal Young licked his lips and watched Shell move behind him. "What are you gonna do?"

"Nothing you won't get over."

Hooking his forefinger into a frayed tear just below Young's collar, he gave it a hard downward tug that staggered the man and ripped half his shirt off. Tearing the material into two strips, he balled up one and crammed as much of it as he could into Young's mouth, then covered his mouth with the second strip to keep him from spitting out the gag and tied the ends tightly together at the nape of his neck. Shell then handcuffed Young's wrists behind his back and relieved him of everything he owned, from wallet to pocketknife, with the swiftness and ease of an expert thief.

Finished, he shoved the trussed-up lawman into the cell and closed and locked the door behind him. Sally watched with solemn interest.

"Now what?" she asked.

Counting the few crinkled greenbacks in Young's wallet, he drew a deep breath. "We wait for Watts."

"Shell . . ."

He glanced over at her.

"We won't have to wait." She was peering out the open door, looking toward the marshal's office a few yards in front. "There he is," she whispered. "Coming out the back way."

Motioning her to stay against the opposite wall, Shell flattened himself inside the doorway, and flipping his gun around so that he was holding it by the barrel, he waited and listened to the crunch of Watts' boots. Across from him, Sally slipped the marshal's gun from its holster, cocked it, and watched the door. There was no time to talk strategy, nor was there any need for it. If Shell missed, she would not.

Jesse Watts spotted Sally the moment he stepped inside the jail but whatever reaction he might have had was left unspoken, for Shell was on him in the same instant, swinging the gun hard against the side of his head. The force of the blow knocked Watts off balance, and he fell against the door facing. When he didn't go down immediately, Shell swung again, this time catching him behind the ear. The bounty hunter's eyes rolled back in his head as his body went limp and slid to the floor.

"Did you kill him?" Sally asked breathlessly.

Shell knelt beside the prone figure, thumbed one eyelid up and looked at the man's pupil, then felt for a pulse. "He's all right."

Sally peered down at Watts over her husband's shoulder. "You nearly cracked his noggin," she said.

As with Marshal Young, Shell searched the bounty hunter, leaving no pocket untouched, and came away with a bowie knife, a handful of loose change, and a money belt that was too heavy not to have something of value inside. He then bound him hand and foot, gagged him, and with Sally's help, dragged him into the cell opposite the marshal's and locked him in. With any luck, the two men wouldn't be found until sometime tomorrow at the earliest. Even then, it would require a hacksaw to get them out. Shell had no intention of leaving the jail keys behind.

Sally stepped outside, and when she was sure no one was around, she motioned to Shell, and they ran across the short stretch of open ground to the marshal's office. The door to the back room was ajar, and they slipped inside and closed it behind them. Walking into the office, Shell locked the front door, glanced out the window at the dusty, near-deserted street, and sagged into a chair.

Sally joined him after a moment and sat on the chair's

arm. Tilting his chin up, she gently sponged his face clean with a wet cloth. "We'll leave tonight?"

"Better. Won't run such a risk of being seen. We'll get us a couple of horses and leave this dry hole behind us for good." He gave her a tired smile. "How does that sound?"

"It sounds fine," she said but didn't return his smile. The excitement over, her face had taken on a serious cast. "You look awful."

"I know. Don't get too close to me. I think I've got cooties."

Sally smiled this time. "I was talking about your black eye and swollen nose. Not your cooties." She drew a ragged breath. "Shell, what are we gonna do? Jesse Watts won't take this laying down, you know."

"Let me worry about Jesse Watts." He took the cloth from her hand, folded it over, and pressed it to a bruise on his cheekbone. The wet coolness felt good. "Why don't you go in the back room and see if Harry has something to eat."

"Hungry?"

"Starving."

Following Sally with his eyes, he watched her leave and tossed the cloth onto Young's cluttered desk. What were they going to do? It was a good question.

He suddenly remembered Jesse Watts' money belt. Picking it up, he leaned forward, cleared a spot on the desk, and emptied the contents of the belt. Out dropped a bright gold coin, then another one, and another, and another.

Shell counted the coins as they fell, then counted them again, unable to believe it. There were thirty-six double eagles. Seven hundred twenty dollars! He glanced up from the pile of coins to see Sally standing in the doorway.

"Take a look at this."

"How much?"

31

"Enough to get us out of Texas, that's for sure."

He ran his fingers through the coins. It was the most money he had seen since his parting with Vic Taylor six years ago. That, too, had been stolen.

He thought it ironic that the harder he worked for money the less he saw of it.

Sally sat on the edge of the desk and looked down at him. "Are you feeling guilty for taking it?" she asked.

"No." He leaned back in his chair, a trace of humor showing in his eyes. "Maybe I should feel guilty for not feeling guilty."

Sally laughed. "So what now? Where will we go?"

"You're going to St. Louis to stay with your sister."

Her smile faded. "Like hell I will. I'm staying with you."

Shell continued as if he hadn't heard. "I'll give you six hundred dollars," he decided. "That'll tide you over until I figure out what to do and send for you."

"I won't do it."

"Come on, Sally. It won't be for long."

Sally's small fists clenched.

He waited, then said, "I thought you liked your sister."

"I do, but you're trying to get rid of me!"

"Shhh!" He glanced out the window. "Keep your voice down."

"Don't change the subject. We're sticking together and that's that. You need me."

"I need to know you're somewhere safe," Shell said.

"Living with Darla and that booze-hound she calls a husband?"

Shell studied her a moment, knowing quite well that he was wasting his time. She would argue the point until he either gave in or they both died of old age. Whichever came first.

He relented. "When you get tired, hot, and dirty, I don't want to hear any complaints."

"You have my word," she said solemnly. "Will we take a train?"

He nodded.

She turned away, walked toward the door opening into Marshal Young's cramped living quarters, then spun back around to look at him.

"Shell, I know you don't like to talk about this," she said, "but I have to ask you something. Have you thought about Laurie and David? If we leave, there won't be anyone to tend to their graves."

Not looking at her, Shell frowned, seeing in his mind the small, lonely graves of their children. David, born so tiny and premature he never had a chance . . . and Laurie. He didn't like to think of her that way, preferring instead to remember the happy little girl tagging behind him while he worked, asking one question after another and wagging a grumpy tomcat around in her arms . . .

"Shell?"

He looked up.

"I don't want to leave them."

"They're not here, Sally."

"Sometimes I wonder. Do you really think there's something better? A heaven, I mean?"

Rising, Shell walked around the desk and drew her to him, stroking her hair.

"I have to," he said.

Leaving Shell in Marshal Young's office, Sally returned to the kitchen and sorted through the meagerly stocked pantry for something to eat. She discovered a can of beans, half a loaf of bread, and a few other odds and ends that might pass for a meal and began her preparations.

Thoughts of Laurie and David plagued Sally's mind. She hoped what Shell had said of them was true, that they were in a better place, for to think otherwise was almost too painful for her to bear. Surely such a short and difficult existence deserved better than a cold grave!

Never had Sally known such heartache as the deaths of her children. For as long as she could remember, she had wished for nothing more than to be a wife and mother and had thought her marriage to Shell the high point of her life . . . until she became pregnant with their first child. To feel the small life growing within her truly exceeded all her expectations of happiness.

But the grueling work she and Shell had shared that first year on their little Texas farm took its toll on Sally, and their baby was born far too early to survive. Sally named her firstborn David and watched him be buried that same day. Stark grief had gripped her soul for months thereafter. This, too, she shared with Shell.

Having learned her lesson in the cruelest way, Sally was more careful in her second pregnancy and no longer helped Shell in the fields, contenting herself to stay at home instead where she prepared their meals, cleaned, and washed and patched Shell's clothes. Indeed, this was enough labor in itself to keep her hustling from dawn till dusk, but she took great pleasure in making Shell happy and comfortable.

Her caution was rewarded by the birth of a healthy baby girl. Laurie Ann Paxton was everything Sally had wished for, a chubby, rosy-cheeked counterpart to the memory of the shriveled little form she and Shell had buried on the small hill behind the house, and all the love they had stored up for their lost son was expelled upon Laurie.

Laurie grew rapidly into a vibrant, curious child who enjoyed nothing more than to follow her father about his daily work with dark, auburn curls bouncing and dusty feet pattering. Shell called her his little shadow and delighted in her company, never caring that she slowed his progress or asked too many questions, and Sally would often stop in her own chores to watch the two of them together. Never in her life had she felt so fulfilled.

Yet in spite of her happiness, a dark cloud of fear of losing either Laurie or Shell never strayed from the back of Sally's mind. Her worries were neither idle nor morbid. Sally's own mother had lost six children, and Shell's entire family had been massacred by Comanches, leaving him an orphan. They had both lived difficult lives, and with the added threat of Shell being wanted by the law, Sally had many reasons to feel anxious.

And so Laurie's sudden illness panicked Sally but did not surprise her. It began with Laurie complaining of a sore throat, which was soon followed by a high fever and a rash upon her back and stomach. Though Shell killed a horse in fetching a doctor from Amarillo, he made it home only to be present during Laurie's final struggling hours. Once again, their hopes and dreams were buried with yet another small child.

Remembering it all with severe clarity, Sally wiped tears from her eyes and sliced the bread she had found in Young's pantry. This then was all her and Shell's hard work and troubles had achieved—half a loaf of stale bread, no home, no children, and a handful of money stolen from a bloodthirsty manhunter who no doubt would be back on their trail come tomorrow morning.

Of course, she had known the risks she had taken marrying a man wanted by the law. Shell had hidden nothing of his past from her during their whirlwind courtship; he had warned her that his deeds as an outlaw might catch up with him someday, yet she saw beyond his faults, saw instead a gentle young man molded by hardship and loss into Vic Taylor's flunky. Confident she could break that mold, Sally agreed to be his wife, and together they had struggled to forge new lives for themselves.

Only to watch it all be buried beneath the parched Texas soil.

Sally sighed, brushed her hair back from her face, and tried to shake the heaviness from her heart. For Shell's sake, she must not appear teary-eyed and gloomy. He needed her, more now than ever.

CHAPTER FOUR

Shell Paxton had a good eye for horseflesh, even in semi-darkness, and the two saddle mounts he took from the corral behind the Lucky Saloon were stayers. He didn't expect to have any trouble getting out of town undetected, but it never hurt to be prepared.

Pushing their horses as hard as they dared, Shell and Sally arrived home shortly before midnight. While Sally hastily threw together a few of their belongings and the little money they had saved up, Shell hitched fresh horses to the wagon and tethered the stolen pair to the tailgate. Once in Amarillo, he would sell the whole outfit.

The couple took one parting look at their house with the moonlight shining on its small, square window panes. They would not see it again, and while it was the first real home Shell had ever known, he couldn't honestly say he was sorry to abandon it. He had accepted the fact that they would have to leave sometime soon anyway.

While Sally rested against his shoulder, he kept the team at a steady jog, and in his mind, hashed out a plan he hoped would rid them of Jesse Watts for good. It would take time and money, but thanks to Watts' distrust in banks, they had plenty of each.

It was nearing dawn when Shell drove past the first houses at the edge of town. Amarillo's city limits had expanded since the last time he had been here. Begun as a construction camp for the crew working on the Fort Worth and Denver City Railroad, Amarillo was now a growing little town and fast becoming a major cattle-shipping point for High Plains ranchers.

The depot was painted a bright, eye-catching yellow, and here Shell bought two second-class tickets for the morning train to Fort Worth.

The agent was a friendly sort, an ex-switchman with three fingers missing from his right hand, and he regarded Shell curiously. "Was it a good one?" he asked suddenly.

"What?"

"The fight you were in, lad. Was it a good one?"

Handing the tickets to Sally, Shell smiled, saying, "No, sir. I lost."

The agent laughed. "You win some, you lose some. It all evens out in the end." He gave Sally a warm smile. "You folks look as if you've been on the road quite a spell. Where do you hail?"

"We've come from Lucky," Shell answered and felt Sally's elbow poke him in the ribs. He ignored her. With any luck, the station agent would remember him well. He was purposely dangling a bone in front of Jesse Watts' nose.

"Been traveling all night," he added innocently.

The agent frowned. "No trouble, I hope."

"No, just bad luck. Creditors got our land, and we're headed back East where we came from."

"You're not alone. Seems like half the country's packing up and moving out. A fella told me the other day that from his place it's a hundred miles to water, fifty miles to wood, and six inches to hell." He shrugged and smiled. "Guess that sums it up, eh?"

The agent seemed to take a particular interest in the young couple, and when Shell mentioned having a wagon and four horses for sale, he introduced him to a man he thought might be interested. After a considerable amount of dickering, Shell was pocketing another fair sum of cash, no questions asked. Normally, men were cautious when buying stock from strangers, especially if the strangers appeared overly anxious to sell, but the horses Shell had taken from Lucky were brandless and there was something about his quiet, straight-forward manner that caused people to instinctively like and trust him. No one suspected he was anything other than what he said he was.

Shell and Sally were the only two passengers boarding the eastbound train. It was nerve-racking, wondering if they would be recognized before they even took their seats. But except for the disturbance two rowdy young cowboys stirred up when they began firing their guns out the open windows at telegraph poles, the trip to Fort Worth passed smoothly, and Shell started catching up on lost sleep. Having ridden the rails only once in her entire life, Sally was too excited to rest.

By the time their train lurched to a stop in Fort Worth, Shell's plan was planted firmly in his mind.

Going by the name of Mr. and Mrs. Jim Roberts, they traveled by train from Fort Worth to Texarkana where they then split up, each taking separate trains at separate times to Little Rock, Arkansas. It wasn't until late the following night before they met again in a sparsely furnished hotel room, and here Shell outlined the final and most crucial part of the plan.

His strategy was fairly simple. Disguising herself and using a false name, Sally would make the long trip to Denver, Colorado, where she would stay with friends, while Shell would serve as a decoy and continue on to St. Louis. Once there, he would buy a horse and head back west again to Colorado where he'd join Sally. By sticking to unsettled country as much as possible, he hoped to lose anyone who might have managed to trail him as far as St. Louis, namely Jesse Watts.

"It'll work," Sally said with conviction and gave Shell a happy smile. "We'll lick him this time."

Looking out the hotel window at the starry sky, Shell

nodded. "Let's hope so."

"Will we stay in Colorado?"

"No." He turned from the window. "How does Arizona sound? I could find a riding job down there, then later we could get a place of our own and buy some stock. Start from scratch."

"Arizona," Sally said softly.

She lay back on the bed and gazed up at the ceiling, long, auburn hair fanned out around her head. She was wearing her summer nightgown. Already sheer, repeated washings had worn it much thinner, and Shell could almost see through it in certain light. He could see enough now to know she was wearing nothing underneath.

Her breasts rose and fell in a deep sigh. "You want to stay near the border, don't you?" she asked.

"Yeah." He prodded himself back to the subject at hand. "Just in case the law . . ."

"Don't say it. I don't even want to think about that. I don't want to think about anything." She rolled her head to the side to look at him. "Not tonight."

Shell pushed away from the window facing and grinned. "So what do you want to do?"

Sitting up, Sally slowly worked her nightgown from beneath her, pulled it over her head, and in the same unhurried manner, let it drop over the side of the bed to the floor.

"Come here, and I'll show you," she said, and her mouth curved in a teasing smile as Shell moved toward her.

Nursing a throbbing headache, Jesse Watts emerged from the Lucky Saloon, paused to light a cigarette, and stepped off the boardwalk to stand beside his horse. Beneath the low, flat brim of his hat, sunken eyes cut to the side, and he saw several men watching him from the open double doorway of the store across the street. One of the men said something, and his friends bobbed their heads in agreement and looked Jesse's way. Somebody laughed.

Hearing the soft, amused chuckle, Jesse Watts turned his head and looked directly at them. The men withdrew, losing themselves in the store's shadowed interior.

Jesse's upper lip curled in disgust as he flicked his cigarette into the street and swung astride his horse.

The long-legged gelding seemed as anxious as Jesse to leave Lucky behind him, but he was held to a dignified walk, and they were half a mile out of town before the pressure on the bit finally eased. He broke into an easy canter.

Jesse Watts' dirty buckskin jacket was of the same drab hue as his mount's uncurried coat, so that the two were one, each blending smoothly in motion and color and all but invisible against the dull backdrop of their surroundings. He slowed the gelding to a trot, and the jarring gait made his head throb all the harder. He welcomed the pain, punishing himself for his carelessness in the handling of Shell Paxton.

Never before had he been so humiliated.

Respect, fear, envy, hatred—these were the common reactions to a manhunter of Jesse Watts' renown, ones he recognized and accepted. But to be laughed at was intolerable.

For two days and a night, he had lain gagged and bound in that pigsty that passed for a jail, and even after he and Marshal Young were found, it had taken hours to saw through the steel bars, giving the whole county ample time to ride in and take a peek at the jailbirds. As if that wasn't enough, the editor of the *Livestock Champion* had ridden out from Amarillo to cover the story personally.

It was a big day for Lucky.

These people seemed to revere Shell Paxton as something of an overnight celebrity, the man who had inadvertently breathed life into Lucky, a feat no one had thought possible since the town was snubbed by the railroad in '87. Jesse's opinion of him was less enthusiastic.

Paxton had a three-day jump on him, and he had taken his wife with him. Not long after his escape, two horses were discovered missing, leading everyone to think the couple intended to flee the country on horseback, perhaps riding south to the border. Though he knew better, Jesse hadn't bothered to discourage the notion. Some simple detective work on his part had revealed that the Paxtons had ridden home where they had packed together a few personal belongings, then had left with a team and wagon, headed not south, but east toward Amarillo. That left only one possibility. They were taking the first train out of Texas.

In an attempt to prove his theory, Jesse tried to follow the wagon tracks, but the trail was too faint, and once it joined the main road, it disappeared beneath a myriad of more recent wagon and hoof prints. Even so, the depot in Amarillo was the obvious destination.

His search would begin there.

CHAPTER FIVE

Central City, Colorado: October, 1888

Cold weather did not agree with Shell Paxton at all. Shivering, he splashed water over his face and head, shaved as quickly as a man could without slitting his throat, and immediately shrugged into a gray flannel shirt and a heavy jacket. Warmer now, he gave his teeth a vigorous brushing and combed down his hair.

Sitting at the foot of the bed with her knees tucked up under her chin, Sally watched her husband perform his usual early morning ritual in half the time it normally took him and shook her head.

"You're the coldest natured person I've ever seen in my life," she teased. "My prince turned out to be a frog."

Tying his shoes, he glanced up at her but made no comment.

"You're awful solemn today," she said.

This, too, seemed to fall upon deaf ears.

His silence was irritating. She padded across the room in her bare feet to stand near the window, curling her toes up away from the chilly floor. This loud, dirty mining town with its loud, dirty men depressed her. It brought to mind too many unpleasant memories.

Sally's father had been a miner in the Colorado goldfields. He was killed when a mine caved in upon him, leaving his wife and two children alone and penniless in a rough camp of two-hundred or more men. Sally's mother, already worn to bones by work and worry, began cooking, sewing, and taking

43

in laundry for the miners in exchange for food and money, and soon became an even paler shadow of herself, a woman with no time or energy for life even, much less two daughters. When she passed away nine years later, Sally did not mourn her passing. She felt her mother had died long ago, a death so gradual no one even realized it was happening, lessening the sudden shock of her loss.

Following their mother's death, Sally's older sister, Darla, declared that she would no longer scrub dirty miner's underdrawers for a living and found them both jobs working in a dance hall called the Silver Buckle. Wearing bright, skimpy dresses that bared their shoulders and legs, they and several other girls were paid to dance with the customers each night. Between times, they waited tables, and if they giggled and flirted enough, a lucky gambler or a prospector who had struck it rich in the mountains might drop a gold coin or two down the fronts of their low-cut dresses. Though only fifteen, Sally had not lived a sheltered life and knew perfectly well what most of the girls did behind closed doors to increase their earnings. Even Darla, she suspected, had done so on more than one occasion, but Sally was too proud for such shenanigans. Most of the men were poor miners anyway, some nice, some not so nice, and she didn't miss working in the Silver Buckle one bit. Nor did she miss living in a mining town.

Remembering the hard times in the mine camps, Sally suddenly turned on Shell. "Tell me the truth. Why are we here?"

"Just for the hell of it."

"Shell, you never do anything just for the hell of it."

He frowned. "What's that supposed to mean?"

"It means you're not impulsive. There's a reason behind everything you do." Her left eyebrow arched, and she gave her bloomers a violent tug. "Including this little last minute jaunt to Central City."

"If you didn't want to come, you should have said so," he told her. "You could have stayed in Denver."

"In case you've forgotten, I haven't seen you in over a month. I wanted to be with you."

Shell straightened his jacket collar and gave her an odd look. "Then why are you complaining?"

"Who's complaining?" Sally burst out. "I'm just trying to get a straight answer out of you!"

Tired of it, Shell dropped into a chair and blew his breath out in a gust.

Watching him, Sally frowned. "You're keeping something from me, aren't you?"

He looked up at her. "If I tell you the truth, you'll just get mad, and I'm not in the mood to argue."

"You never are," she said. "Now spit it out."

He shrugged. "It's Vic."

Sally's face fell.

"He's here," Shell continued. "Or he will be soon."

"How do you know?"

"When I got to Denver, I met up with one of the fellas I used to run with before we were married. Eladio Diaz. Remember him? He told me he'd talked to Vic a day or two ago and that he was headed here. He'll be stopping over at Leo Moffat's saloon."

Sally didn't bother to hide her disappointment. "Shell, why? Why do you insist on keeping him in our lives?" She knelt down in front of him and folded her arms across his knees, her eyes searching his face. He wouldn't look at her. "Please, Shell, let's just leave."

"I wanted to see him," he said quietly. "I thought he might help us out, maybe give me some advice."

Sally gazed up at him, feeling almost sad. Shell had spent so many years of his life being told what to do that it was difficult for him to do anything on his own.

"Then go talk to him," she said at length. "Just don't tell him we're going to Arizona, all right? Please?"

Shell finally looked down at her. "Why do you hate him so much?"

"I hate the control he has over you. Every time he visited us in Texas, it was the same way. He'd talk you into joining him in one of his grand schemes, and I'd have to work twice as long and hard to talk you out of it." Pausing, she watched him, making sure he was still listening. "You had a home and a baby girl to think about then, and it was easier to keep you with us where you belonged. But now that it's just me . . ." She shook her head. "I don't know if I'm enough."

Smiling a little, Shell leaned forward and gently held her face between his hands. She felt the hard callouses on his palms pressing against her cheeks.

"You're plenty," he said, "so stop worrying."

Her face brightened. "Then let's leave. Right now." She hopped to her feet and cast a quick look around their hotel room. "I can have our things packed in a jiffy."

Shell stared at her. "Sally, you don't get it, do you?" He got up and walked slowly to the door. Resting a hand on the knob, he turned to look back at her. "The man raised me, and you want me to just forget he exists. I can't do it."

Biting her lower lip, Sally watched him step out into the hall and silently close the door behind him.

She didn't know whether to be mad at him or not. Why couldn't he just yell and cuss and slam doors like everyone else? At least she would know how to react.

Standing with her face close to the window pane, she looked down on Eureka Street. She had no trouble spotting

Shell, for he was one of the few men on the sidewalk not wearing a hat. He ran across the busy street, white steam puffing from his mouth, and Sally watched him until he passed from sight. She had half a mind to follow him but decided against it. Her presence wouldn't change anything. He would see Vic no matter what.

Shell's devotion to the man was genuine and deep felt, and in a way, Sally understood why.

Though Shell rarely mentioned it, Vic had told her the story—how Shell's mother and father and older brother had been murdered by Comanches in the Elm Creek raid of 1864. Shell had been only four years old, and his mother had hidden him in the brush when the Indians struck, and it was on that beautiful autumn day that he lost his entire family.

After that, Shell was sent to live with his Aunt Myra in East Texas who hired him out to work for her neighbors. Amounting to little more than cheap labor, he had been treated badly, and Sally guessed it was no wonder he looked upon Vic Taylor as his savior.

An old friend of the Paxtons' and a wandering rogue, Vic rescued Shell from there when he was twelve and took him straight to the California boom towns. Forget the three R's. Instead, Shell was schooled in the fine art of thievery and eventually graduated from picking cotton to picking pockets, handing over three-fourths of everything he stole to Vic.

Thanks to Vic Taylor, Shell's innocence was soon lost, and now he had a price on his head, and the law on his trail, and Sally could not convince him that Vic was largely to blame.

Suddenly remembering that Vic, too, was worth a sizable sum of money, Sally smiled to herself. She almost wished there was some way she could turn him in to the law.

She and Shell could do a lot with three thousand dollars.

★ ★ ★ ★ ★

The gold mining town of Central City was jammed down between two ugly, pockmarked mountains with a stream of muddy water rushing down the middle of it. Houses rested on high posts or scaffolding over the stream's deep bed, most of them looking as if they were standing on shaky legs. On the other side of the water was a narrow, wandering, potholed street that climbed steadily up the bottom of the gulch to the next crowded mining town of Nevadaville, some nine thousand feet above sea level and the highest of the string of settlements along Gregory's Gulch.

With all the blasting and digging that went on in the search for mineral wealth, mining districts were never picturesque, but there was always plenty to see and hear and smell. Puffs of steam and smoke, the dull thumping of the stamp mills, men's voices, and the sounds of all manner of machinery filled the air, yet even with all this activity, the boom days of Central City were on the decline.

The town no longer had such a temporary appearance. Flimsy, wooden structures hastily slapped together in the early years had burned to the ground and been replaced by impressive stone and brick buildings. And there were more women than Shell remembered, women with families this time of all nationalities. A flat-chested, slim-hipped Chinese girl sprinted by with a load of laundry, ducking her head as she passed as if she expected Shell to strike her.

Shell had been dizzy with a headache all day yesterday, and though he was growing used to the high altitude, he was still a little out of breath by the time he reached the edge of town. Pausing in front of a familiar two-story building with no sign or anything to suggest it might be a place of business, he glanced up at the sky. It was ash gray, promising to send down this winter's first snow very soon, possibly tonight.

He'd be glad to get to southern Arizona where it was warmer.

He looked back at the building in front of him. Yes, this was the place. Leo Moffat's saloon. He remembered it well. He and Vic and Eladio Diaz and others of their old gang had met here more than once when life in California got too exciting for comfort. The saloon was frequented by the district's rougher crowd and served as a safe haven for men like himself who were slightly wayward of the law. He opened the door and stepped inside.

Cold air and cigarette smoke mixed together within bad lungs made for a miserable situation so he breathed shallow, taking in a little air at a time, conditioning his lungs to their new environment as he moved toward the bar. The place was almost empty. Two patrons stood together at one end of the crude, plank bar, smoking and drinking and watching Shell from beneath lowered brows, not moving their heads. One was a dirty-blond with a pimply, pitted face and peach fuzz showing on his upper lip. The other was taller and older and balding, with a body that seemed to start in the middle and taper down at both ends. Having noticed that much in the few seconds it took him to walk to the bar, Shell dismissed them and smiled at the short, stocky man who was drying a chipped glass and squinting at him through nearsighted eyes.

"How you doing, Leo?"

Still staring at him, Leo Moffat drew closer. "Well, I'll just be damned," he said and thrust out a hand. "Shell, it's good to see you."

He wrung Shell's hand, grinning from ear to ear, a rarity where Leo Moffat was concerned, and shook his head as if he couldn't believe it. After all these years. Shell said, yes, it had been a long time, and though he had never seen the woman in his life, asked how Mrs. Moffat was doing, out of politeness. The mention of his wife brought forth Leo's customary scowl.

49

"Nag, nag, nag," he said and dismissed her with a wave of his cup towel. "What can I get you, Shell? How does brandy sound?"

"Too early for me. Coffee sounds better."

Leo nodded and ambled over to the old Black Prince cookstove in the corner of the saloon where a fresh pot of coffee was keeping warm.

"Sugar?"

"No thanks."

Leo set the coffee on the bar in front of Shell and gave him a sly look. "Getting your sugar at home, eh? How is Sally anyway?"

"She's fine."

"Good. That's good." Leo rested an arm on the bar and leaned toward Shell. "I don't guess I have to ask why you're here."

Shell sipped his coffee and glanced up at him. "I was looking for Vic."

"He's upstairs, sleeping off a drunk."

"That right?"

"Got rip-roaring drunk last night," Leo said. "Thought he was going to tear the place up 'fore he finally passed out. Took four men to carry him upstairs and dump him in bed."

Not surprised, Shell merely nodded, took another swallow of coffee. Vic rarely drank, but when he did, he made up for the dry spells.

"You know what he did last time he was here?" Leo asked.

"Vic? There's no telling."

Leo leaned closer and lowered his voice. "He was resting up from one of his benders, like he's doing now, only this was a bad one," he said and rolled his eyes to the ceiling. "He'd been up there two days, not a sound out of him all that time, and I got to thinking, Hell's fire, if the bloody fool's dead, he'll start stinking up the place. So I says to this fellow working for me, 'Jimbo, why don't you go up and see if he's still breathing.' Jimbo goes, and you know what Vic does?"

Shell didn't know.

"He hits Jimbo over the head with the chamber pot, busts the poor bloke's skull wide open. Like a ripe watermelon, you might say."

This time, Shell was surprised. "Killed him?"

"Hell, yeah, it killed him. Brains everywhere. Never seen such a mess." He jabbed his forefinger against the bar. "Blood dripped down between the boards into old Doc Harder's whiskey glass. Damn fool was so drunk he never knew the difference."

"When was this?"

"Four, five months ago. Vic thought he was a thief."

"Anyone report the killing?"

"No, we kept it quiet," Leo said. "Anyway, he claimed it was self-defense, and I didn't argue. Jimbo never was real bright, you know. Maybe he did try to lift something, thinking Vic was asleep or too hung over to notice."

Shell nodded, although the punishment seemed a bit excessive, considering Vic was a thief, too.

Leo slapped him on the arm. "I'll go wake him up. He'll be tickled to see you."

"Be careful."

Laughing, Leo refilled Shell's cup and carried the coffee pot upstairs.

Shell turned his back to the bar, drinking his coffee and looking around him. Nothing ever changed here. Leo was the same and so was his saloon, everything rough and plain and relaxed, the way he liked it.

He thought about Vic. He hadn't seen him in over a year and couldn't shake the tight queasiness inside his stomach.

Shell could care less what other men thought of him, but with Vic it was a different matter. Like a child eager to please a demanding parent, he worried that Vic would find fault with him, worried that he'd criticize his handling of Jesse Watts.

He hadn't been completely honest with Sally. More than Vic's advice, he needed his reassurance that he was making the right moves. And why shouldn't he look to Vic for that? Before he married, this one man was as close to family as Shell had known since he was a young boy, and it wasn't easy for him, even now, to sever that tie. Vic Taylor had done more than raise him. He had taught him how to survive.

Shell had turned back to the bar and was aware that one of the two men at the end was becoming drunker and louder. He glanced up to look at the head of the stairs, wondering if Leo was having trouble rousing Vic out of bed, or if he had gotten his brains bashed out with a chamber pot. He'd give them a few more minutes.

"Hey, Joe, will you look at this?"

Shell glanced around. Gripping the neck of the whiskey bottle in his right hand, the pock-faced kid was gazing out the window.

"Come take a look at this hombre," he said.

Joe looked. "Now there's a mail-order cowboy if ever I seen one."

Shell saw a man in a big, snow white hat walk past the saloon with his thumbs tucked in his pants' pockets. Decked out in fancy chaps with conchas up the sides, high-heeled, Mexican boots, and that ridiculous hat, he appeared very much out of place in a town full of black-faced miners wearing denim and brogans.

The blond kid grinned and swaggered back to the bar to join his friend. "Maybe the Wild West Show's in town, and we weren't invited."

"Nah." Joe tossed off his drink. "Probably some damn Texan," he said loudly, his words slurred. "Texans are funny that way. If they own five cows, they think they're cattle barons."

The blond kid appeared interested. "I never been to Texas."

"You ain't missed nothin'."

Smiling faintly, Shell lifted his cup, about to take a drink, when he became aware that the surly Joe who hated Texans was eyeing him from the end of the bar.

"Hey, you. What the hell're you grinnin' about? Somebody pull your string?"

It took Shell by surprise, but he didn't show it. His coffee cup still poised, he looked over at Joe and in a natural drawl that was unmistakably Texan, said, "No, I reckon nobody did."

"You hear that, Darby?" Joe turned to face Shell, holding on to the edge of the bar to steady himself. "Sounds like we got one of them Lone Star chuckleheads right here in the same room with us."

Darby grinned, enjoying it. Shell figured he was around sixteen or seventeen, a big boy who was feeling his oats.

"Who are you anyway?" he asked Shell. "You don't look like one of us."

Shell started to thank him but changed his mind. No sense in getting nasty. Instead, he put on a friendly smile and said, "Is that right?" and drained his cup.

Darby's eyes narrowed. "Wait a minute. You ain't the law, are you?"

"Leo'd kicked his ass out the front door if he was a lawdog," Joe said and glared at Shell through a drunken haze. "Buy us a drink, Texas."

"Looks to me like you've had plenty already," Shell said,

still polite but not smiling now.

Darby studied him intently, and his gaze held for a moment on Shell's holstered Colt before moving back up to his face. No longer interested, Joe slopped more whiskey into his glass, spilling some on the bar.

Darby said, "Mister, I don't like your looks."

CHAPTER SIX

Shell wondered how many times the kid had rehearsed that line. Standing in front of a mirror, hands hanging loose at his sides and barely touching the walnut grips of his holstered guns, saying, "Mister, I don't like your looks," in a low, even voice that sounded good in his ears.

Shell Paxton was a tolerant man. He had seen his share of bullies, drunks, and tough, smart-mouthed kids with just enough bad whiskey sloshing around in their stomachs to make them do something stupid, and he had never had too much trouble with any of them, mainly because he rarely lost his temper.

It was no different today.

"Darby, you know something?" he said. "You look to me like a nice boy."

Darby stared at him.

"I'm serious," Shell went on. "That's why I'm gonna give you some advice. Don't pick fights with people you don't know nothing about. You might get more than you asked for." He gestured casually to the near-empty bottle of rotgut in front of Joe. "And if you can't afford good whiskey, then don't buy any. That crap you got there'll eat your insides out before you hit voting age if you drink too much of it."

Joe dragged a hand down his face and cast a sidelong look at Darby. "Didn't I tell you Texans talked too much?"

Darby was still staring at Shell, slightly bewildered, seeing the man actually turn his back on him as Vic Taylor and Leo Moffat came clumping down the stairs. It was humiliating, and there wasn't a thing he could do about it. So he left.

★ ★ ★ ★ ★

Vic didn't look like a man who had just crawled out of bed.

He and Shell were sitting across from each other at a table near the stove, sipping their coffee and watching Leo set out mouse traps in various strategic locations around the saloon. Before coming down, Vic had shaved and put on a clean, bright red shirt, and his salt and pepper hair was slicked back smoothly from his forehead, showing off his widow's peak. His mustache was a little heavy, having not been trimmed recently, but other than that Shell thought he looked fit as ever for a man who was crowding sixty. All two hundred fifty muscle-packed pounds of him.

Vic caught his gaze and smiled. "You're a good boy, Shell."

"What makes you say that?"

"Coming to check up on the old man when you've got problems of your own."

Shell waited for him to elaborate on that.

"I've been reading about you in the newspapers."

Shell gave him a quick look. "You what?"

Vic's leathery face spread horizontally in a wide grin. "You're famous, kid. You didn't know that?" He dipped two fingers into a hidden pocket on the inside of his vest, drew out a small, worn Bible and opened it. A folded newspaper clipping dropped out onto the table. Holding it up to the light filtering through the window, his eyes moved rapidly back and forth, then stopped halfway down the article. "Says right here: 'Paxton gave local law authorities the slip August 15, stealing two horses belonging to the Lucky Livery Stable and over one thousand dollars in gold specie. He and his wife are believed to be traveling together, and officials speculate that the fugitives may be headed for Mexico. Any information leading to the arrest of Shelvin Paxton . . .' " Vic's voice trailed off, and his eyes darted back to the beginning of the article. "Here it is," he said. "The best part: 'Paxton is the first prisoner known to escape the clutches of the well-known manhunter and should be considered armed and dangerous.' "

"Jesus."

Vic laughed. "You're looking a little green around the gills, Shell. You feel all right?"

"I didn't know it made the papers. Why didn't Eladio say something the other day?"

"He's like you. Never learned to read."

"Or Leo."

Vic struck a match and touched it to a corner of the paper, dropping both into a spittoon. "Leo reads dime novels and whiskey labels. Not newspapers."

Still stunned, Shell asked, "What paper was that from?"

"Picked it up in Las Vegas, New Mexico. None of the Colorado newspapers I've seen have mentioned you."

"Good." Shell glanced up at him. "It was a little over seven hundred dollars, by the way, not a thousand."

Vic shrugged. "Editors like good solid-sounding figures."

"Speaking of figures, did you know you're worth three thousand?"

"So I've heard."

Vic reached into a paper bag peeking over the top of his shirt pocket and flipped a lemon drop into his mouth. Vic Taylor had a wicked sweet tooth. Shell had never seen him smoke or chew tobacco, and he could go for months without a drop of liquor, but take away his sugar supply, and he'd kill you.

Vic rolled the lemon drop to his left cheek and regarded Shell fondly. "Made any plans?"

"We're going to Arizona."

"You'll never make it," Vic said bluntly. "You might get a
year of grace, maybe even two if you're lucky, but Watts or
somebody else'll corner you before it's over. Just like in
Texas." He bit into the lemon drop with a hollow crunch.
"You know why?"

Shell waited.

"Two reasons. Sally and Laurie. No disrespect, but
they're like anchors around your neck."

Shell didn't bother to inform him that there was one less
anchor. "If it hadn't been for Sally," he said, "I'd still be in
jail."

Vic smiled. "If it hadn't been for Sally, you'd still be with
me, riding the backtrails, seeing the sights, and robbing the
rich to feed the poor. Free as a bird, Shell. Think about it."

"I have," Shell said, "and I'm through. I'm staying
straight."

"Is that why you picked those boys' pockets clean before
you flew the coop?"

Shell frowned. "That was different. We needed money to
put some distance between us and Jesse Watts."

"You still do." Folding his arms on the table, Vic leaned
toward him, his face serious. "Two things can happen to you
in Arizona. The law will either corner you and kill you or
they'll pack your ass off to prison. Do you know what all goes
on in the pen? What if some big Nancy-boy sets his cap for
you, decides he wants you for his gal? What the hell are you
gonna do about it?"

"Get to the point, Vic."

"My point is, keep out of prison."

"That's what I'm trying to do."

"No, you're not. You're trying to settle down and raise a
family and that's gonna get you a one-way trip to San

Quentin. What you need to do," he said, "is get enough money in your pockets that you don't have to work another day of your life, then take your family and get out of the country. Mark my words, Shell, it's the only way."

Shell considered what he had said, taking his time. Vic was long-winded, and as usual, was talking circles around him. He wondered what all this was leading up to.

"When money starts growing on trees," he said after a moment, "be sure and tell me."

Vic grinned. "Forget the damned trees. I know where there's eight gold ingots just waiting for somebody to pick 'em up."

"Is that a fact?" Shell kept his voice bland.

Vic noticed it and shook his head in disgust. "I see Sally's been working on you again. Got you tame as a dead squirrel. Eight seventy-five pound ingots, Shell. That'd assay out to about two hundred thousand dollars, give or take a little. Doesn't that make your blood rush?"

"It would if I had it right here in front of me and knew it was mine."

"That gold's as good as ours," Vic declared.

"What's the catch?"

"We have to find it."

"I thought you said you knew where it was."

"I know its approximate whereabouts."

Puzzled, Shell studied him intently. "Is this lost gold you're talking about? Hidden treasure?"

Vic nodded, his eyes sparkling with either greed or excitement, Shell wasn't sure which. Knowing Vic, probably both.

"Aren't you a little old for fairy tales?" he asked.

"This is the real thing, kid. I've checked it out." Vic drained his coffee cup and held it out to Leo as he passed by their table. "Did I ever tell you about an old friend of mine? Malo Chavez?"

Shell thought a minute, then shook his head. "If you did, I've forgot."

"Malo Chavez used to be one of the most feared *bandidos* to cross the border."

"That sounds like one of your friends, all right," Shell said sarcastically.

Vic laughed. "Damned right. Bastard taught me everything I know." He grew serious. "Down in New Mexico, just west of Elizabethtown, there used to be a working mine called the Last Chance. From what I've gathered it produced a lot of ore for several years. There was some trouble packing that gold over the mountains to Santa Fe on account of Chavez and his gang. One mule train never made it a'tall. The whole party was killed and left for the coyotes." Vic suddenly grinned. "Eight gold ingots were stolen."

"What happened then?"

"Adam Chaney, the owner of the Last Chance, gathered up some men and went after them. Trailed the bandits several days, got caught in a snowstorm and had to turn back." Vic shifted his candy to the opposite cheek. "That next year, after the spring thaw, Chaney found a few human bones in a place called Devil's Canyon and figured they were all that was left of Chavez's men. Nobody ever knew if any of the gang made it through that winter, and nobody knew what happened to the gold. Until now, that is." Vic dipped his head toward the bar where Joe, the Texan hater, was nodding over his whiskey glass. "Those two you were talking with before I came down—Joe Finney and Darby James—they hit me up a few weeks ago and started quizzing me about Chavez, asking me if I used to be a friend of his. I told 'em, 'Yeah, but Malo's been dead for nigh onto twenty years.' "

"And?"

Vic smiled. "Would you believe that skinny old Mex has been living with his wife and two dozen brats down in Mexico all these years?"

"How do you know?"

"Joe Finney told me."

"So Chavez made it out with the gold after all, huh?"

"Not exactly," Vic said. "After I found out Malo was alive, I went to see him. His wife died last year, and he's living in the ghost town now where the Last Chance Mine used to be. He told me what happened:

"When him and his men got caught in that blizzard, they found a small cave in Devil's Canyon and tried to wait it out, then another storm blew in and so on until they wound up having to eat their horses and mules to keep from starving to death." Vic paused, frowning. "Malo tells me the only reason he survived was because he ate the bodies of his partners who died from starvation or the cold. Can you imagine that?" He looked at Shell and shook his head, slowly. "Anyhow, he buried the gold in that cave, struck out by himself after one of the storms, and lived to tell one heck of a story."

"He never went back for his gold?" Shell asked.

"No. He's scared to." Vic winked at him. "Malo's a superstitious old man. He tells me Devil's Canyon is haunted. There've been several men to search for that gold and some of 'em didn't come back alive. And them that do come back tell tales of strange things happening. Gear coming up missing, horses and mules acting spooky for no apparent reason, freak accidents. Malo says it's the ghosts of his friends protecting that stolen gold. You know what I think?"

"What?"

"I think Adam Chaney's behind it all."

Vic went on to tell him what he knew about Chaney. The man was as much a crook as Malo Chavez. He had gained full ownership of the Last Chance after the strange disappearances of both his partners. Neither man was ever found, and while foul play was strongly suspected, it could not be proven.

The Last Chance gold mine made Adam Chaney a rich man, but a series of bad investments, gambling losses, and slick-talking swindlers depleted his fortune, and then his mine played out. By the end of the 1870s, he was penniless. His real last chance now lay hidden in Devil's Canyon. By rights, the gold belonged to him, and he had been searching for it for several years.

"Malo told me that as soon as Chaney found out he was alive he started threatening him, claiming he'd kill him if he didn't show him where the gold is."

"He wants it pretty bad, I guess," Shell said.

Vic nodded. "Bad enough to kill for it. So does Malo, but he's scared to set foot in Devil's Canyon, and until I came along, he never trusted anyone to get it for him."

Shell's brows lifted. "You're telling me he trusts you?"

"Exactly. We worked out an agreement a few weeks ago," Vic told him. "If I find the bullion, I've agreed to give him half. We shook hands on it, and he drew me a good map."

"I see."

A slow smile spread across Vic's broad face when he saw the doubt in Shell's eyes. "You don't believe me?"

"It sounds too good to be true, that's all."

"I'll bet you two hundred thousand dollars it isn't," Vic said with a smile.

Watching him, Shell thought about all he had said. The ease with which he had gained Chavez's trust, a map, and his blessings was characteristic of him. Vic Taylor could talk a snake out of its rattles if he so wished.

The story he had related was not unlike a dozen others Shell had heard. There was the Lost Dutchman Mine in Arizona, Pegleg Smith's Lost Gold out in California, and New Mexico's Lost Adams Diggings. All were fabulous, much-exaggerated tales, and while Shell found them interesting, he wasn't a true believer. Yet Vic's enthusiasm served to pique his interest a step further. It wasn't like the big man to waste time and energy on something unless he knew it was worth the effort. Shell was beginning to believe.

"You're really going after it?" he asked.

Vic nodded. "Next spring."

"You mentioned Darby James and Joe Finney . . ."

"Joe knew me and Malo used to be friends," Vic explained. "He offered me a share of the gold if I'd help him and Darby get the old man to tell where it's stashed."

Shell's gaze touched Joe Finney, then settled back on Vic. "You trust them?"

Vic swore softly. "Are you kidding me?" He scowled. "I don't trust them, and they don't trust me, but I figured it'd be smarter to have them come along so's I can keep an eye on them. And anyway, I hear Devil's Canyon takes in some pretty rough country, so I'll probably need their help getting the gold out." He leaned toward Shell and lowered his voice. "Your meeting me here in Colorado is a godsend."

"I don't follow you."

"Joe Finney, Darby James, and me. Two against one. I need somebody I can trust to side me because if we find that bullion, it's gonna be dog-eat-dog all the way to Mexico."

"You're selling it in Mexico, huh?"

"Sure. I know several folks south of the border who'll buy it and keep their mouths shut." Vic paused momentarily, studying him. "So how about it? Are you with me?"

Shell idly counted the upturned whiskey glasses lined up in a row on the bar and thought about those eight gold bars buried somewhere in Devil's Canyon. He glanced at Vic. "I don't know."

Vic slammed his fist down on the table, and Shell flinched in spite of himself. "You think I've been telling you all this to hear my head rattle?" He looked at Shell fiercely. "I need your help."

"I'd like to think about it first," Shell said quietly.

"What's there to think about? Listen to me. There's two hundred thousand dollars there for the taking. Now here's the way I've got it figured. We'll give Joe and Darby a small share, say a thousand apiece, enough to make it worth their while. That'd leave us with . . . What? You're the 'rithmatic expert."

"One hundred ninety-eight thousand dollars," Shell replied.

Vic grinned. "You and me will split that right down the middle. What does that come to?"

"Ninety-nine thousand apiece. But you forgot your pal, Malo. I thought he was supposed to get half."

Vic rolled his eyes skyward. "What's a half-blind, seventy-eight year old man with rheumatism gonna do with that much money?"

"Maybe he'll buy himself a pair of spectacles and hire some good-lookin' *señorita* to take care of him," Shell said and smiled. "The point is, you made an agreement with him, and you ought to keep it."

Vic merely shrugged. "That's the difference between you and me," he said. "You've got a conscience, and I don't. But I'll give what you said some thought if you'll throw in with me."

"Joe and Darby won't like it."

"So?" Vic brushed them aside. "Look, Shell, I know the gold's there. It's just a matter of getting it out. I need some-

body I can trust to side me, and you're the man for the job."
He reached out and gripped Shell's shoulder so hard it hurt.
"You got no home, no money, no rich kinfolk. You're poor as
a hind-tit calf. What've you got to lose?"

"When you put it that way, not much."

"So can I count on you?"

When he didn't answer immediately, Vic's hand tightened
on his shoulder, the thick, square fingers digging into him as
deeply as his grip of authority. Shell didn't flinch or try to pull
away, but there was a sudden tenseness in him, and he remembered the time when he was a boy and Vic caught him
holding back swag he had weeded from a rich dupe's wallet.
Vic had beaten the living hell out of him. Shell knew he was
too old to be whipped into submission, but there was still that
feeling.

And it wasn't as if he didn't need the money.

Eyes lowered, he slowly nodded. "I guess you can count
me in."

"Good! That's more like it!"

The heavy hand on Shell's shoulder lifted, yet he could
still feel the weight of it.

Vic beamed, displaying the wide gap between his two front
teeth, and yelled at Leo to break out the cognac. This called
for a celebration.

He turned back to Shell. "As soon as we get a couple of
drinks under our belts, I'll send somebody to the hotel to es-
cort your pretty little woman back here, and we'll tell her the
good news. Then we'll make our winter plans."

Shell glanced up at him, frowning slightly. "Winter
plans?"

"Sure. We need money to see us through till spring," Vic
explained. "Now, there's a shipment of gold due . . ."

"No way." Shell shook his head, not liking where this was

leading. "I'm not doing anymore hold-up jobs. I'm through with that kind of life."

Vic's face hardened. "That kind of life," he said, spacing out the words. He stabbed a finger at him. "You listen to me, and you listen good. It was that kind of life that kept food in your belly and clothes on your back when you were a scrawny, snot-nosed kid. It was that kind of life that got you out of the cottonfields."

Vic leaned back in his chair and drew a long breath. "If you're coming with me next spring to hunt for the Last Chance gold, you'll damned well pull your share of the weight. There's no telling how long it'll take us to find it, so we'll need money for supplies, and we'll need good, sound horses and pack animals. Given the fact you're one of the best horse thieves in the country, I'll assign that job to you."

Feeling drained, Shell stared out the window and slowly sipped his cognac. It lit a fire in his gut and served to burn away the tight knot.

"I need to tell Sally," he said. "Alone."

Pleased, Vic tossed off his drink and wiped his mustache dry on the back of his hand. "You do that, son."

CHAPTER SEVEN

Jesse Watts relished a challenge.

Slippery outlaws, twisting trails, and shadowy clues were what kept his job interesting, and his pursuit of Shell Paxton had entailed all this and more since he first decided to take up the chase a year ago.

Following the jailbreak, however, Jesse's search became relatively easy, and he half-expected to have Paxton in cuffs and leg-irons before the end of the month. Ask for a quiet-mannered young man under medium height and a pretty girl with long, auburn hair, flash a reward dodger, and tongues wagged all the way from Amarillo to Wichita Falls. Most of the agents and clerks he spoke to seemed surprised that their "nice, polite young feller" was actually wanted for armed robbery. Technically, Sally Paxton could be arrested for helping her husband escape, but Jesse doubted the charge would hold up in court, and so long as there wasn't a price on her head, he wasn't interested. Paxton was his prey, and it wasn't just for the bounty anymore. Jesse had his own personal score to settle.

By the time he reached Fort Worth, the trail had grown cold and memories were vague. Jesse puttered around the Texas cow town for three days, questioning station agents, hotel clerks, the marshal, livery keepers, and anyone else he thought Shell Paxton might have come into contact with, all to no avail. On the afternoon of the third day, however, his luck finally turned.

He had seen the old woman hobbling around the train depot off and on ever since his arrival, peddling homemade rolls, muffins, and cookies to hungry passengers. Grasping for straws, he described Shell and Sally Paxton to her and saw her shriveled face brighten. She remembered them all right. Such a nice couple. She had gone inside the depot, out of the hot sun, and Paxton had bought something from her. She remembered him well because he had overpaid and when she started to count out his change, he told her to keep it. That didn't happen often, she said, and she never forgot anyone who did her a good turn. She remembered them in her prayers. Jesse advised her not to waste her breath.

On further questioning, he learned that the woman had overheard Paxton asking for tickets to Texarkana and immediately made plans to go there himself. Tired of riding with the hoboes in empty boxcars, he hit up a friend in Fort Worth for a grubstake, bought a train ticket, and headed out again after a four-day delay.

But his man was starting to cover his trail now, and early suspicions Jesse had kept smothered rose to the surface. Normally, an outlaw on the dodge spent the first few days trying to lose his pursuers, then little by little he might grow less cautious, figuring he had put enough distance between himself and the law to be safe. Shell Paxton's strategy was the reverse. He hadn't made any effort in the beginning to disguise who he was and had slipped up twice by mentioning tidbits of personal information to ticket agents in both Amarillo and Quanah. Or were these slip-ups?

Jesse had the distinct feeling he was being led on a wild goose chase.

Having reached an impasse in Texarkana, he took time out to reassess what he knew about Shell and Sally Paxton. Paxton's stomping grounds were west of Texas, not east. He had friends out there, men who would help him out in a pinch, and Jesse thought it unlikely that Paxton would want to distance himself from them, particularly now. He suspected Shell Paxton had deliberately led him this far east in order to throw him off course, then somewhere along the way, had quietly doubled back.

On the other hand, there were the letters he had found while searching the Paxtons' house. A whole bundle of them tied together with a pink ribbon had been tucked away in a bureau drawer, all of them addressed to Sally Paxton from a Darla Jewell of St. Louis, the most recent one postmarked June 20. Jesse had scanned enough of the letters to discern that Darla was Sally's sister and had prudently tucked one of the envelopes bearing a return address into his pocket . . . just in case.

Was that where they had headed? St. Louis? It was possible, and even if they hadn't gone anywhere near the place, it might be worth his while to check out this Darla Jewell. Certainly there was nothing keeping him here. Having already questioned enough people in and around Texarkana to populate a fair-sized town and with no luck, Jesse was ready to try anything. He caught the first train to Missouri.

Smoke stacks, elevators, sooty skies, and noise greeted Jesse's eyes and ears when he stepped off the train at the Union Depot, and while there was much to see and do in St. Louis, he couldn't wait to get his business finished and get out. This bustling French city was too much for him.

Feeling dirty and rank, Jesse wasted no time in cleaning up and changing into something more suited to the city. Trimmed up, decked out, and reeking of bay rum, he melted into the crowd.

With the help of James B. Hume, a detective working for Wells Fargo in California, a special arrangement was made with the postmaster to have a surveillance placed on Robert and Darla Jewell's mail. If any suspicious-looking letters showed up, he was to be notified immediately. In the meantime, he did some detective work of his own.

The Jewells owned a small boardinghouse near the levee on Carondelet Street. Here, amidst the pounding of triphammers and the roar of air blasts and circular saws—St. Louis in all its industrial glory—the Jewell family eked out their meager living. Across the narrow street in a vacant building, Jesse Watts waited and watched.

For two weeks, he saw boarders leave in the morning for the nearby steel mill where they worked, and each evening, he watched these same men return for supper and bed. Two of the Jewells' three children walked to and from school. Darla, a tired, older version of her sister, went shopping for groceries with a toddler in tow, and Robert Jewell ducked into the grog shop and sometimes didn't stagger home until after midnight. If Shell and Sally Paxton were here, they were keeping a mighty low profile.

A hole worn in his patience, Jesse was climbing the walls by the end of the first week and was convinced he had been wrong to come here by the middle of week two. He knew every face of every man, woman, and child on this whole street and none of them were the ones he was searching for.

Then he got the news. A letter bearing no return address had been mailed to Darla Jewell, postmarked Denver, Colorado. This could be it.

Standing in the mail room of the gray granite post office on Olive Street, Jesse tugged at his collar and tie, unused to the constraints a suit and collar could place on a man's breathing, and turned the sealed envelope over in his hands.

He glanced over at the man across from him. "I'll be keeping this."

"You can't do that," the postmaster objected. "It's against regulations."

"Mister, don't try shoving your city slicker rules down my throat. There's a sight too many to swallow."

The postmaster's eyes bulged. "Tampering with the U.S. mail is a federal offense!" His voice was shrill.

The letter still in his hand, Jesse glanced around the mail room. It was late, and they were alone. With his free hand, he grasped a handful of the postmaster's shirt in his fist and almost lifted him off the floor.

"No little squeaky-clean milksop tells me what to do. Understand that?"

The postmaster said no more as Jesse ripped into the envelope and unfolded the two-page letter. It was from Sally Paxton.

Scanning her small, neat handwriting, he picked out the salient details and smiled to himself. So Paxton had come here to St. Louis, after all. His wife was waiting for him in Denver. Jesse glanced at the date on the envelope and frowned. September. Depending on how fast he traveled, Paxton might already be in Colorado.

No matter. The letter held valuable information, and Jesse reminded himself to never underestimate the young outlaw again.

Shell Paxton had tried to pull a fast one on him and had come very close to succeeding.

CHAPTER EIGHT

Shell had been eyeing the emerald stickpin off and on ever since their stage rolled out of Burkville half an hour ago. The green stone gleamed above the collar of its owner's high-buttoned overcoat, catching Shell's eye, and he wondered if it was genuine. He supposed he would find out soon enough. Before this trip was over, it would be his.

The emerald wasn't the only eye-catching object within the crowded confines of the Burkville-Dillon stagecoach. His fellow passengers were a diverse bunch. Directly across from him in the front seat was an attractive, red-haired girl who looked like a permanent resident of one of the fancy cathouses back in Burkville, and she took no pains to hide the fact, nor anything else for that matter. Despite the bitter cold, her coat was open, revealing a plunging neckline and a lot of smooth white skin. Her breasts were pushed high and squeezed together, creating cleavage she might not have had otherwise. Each time she bent over, Shell was certain one or both would spring free of the flimsy material of her dress.

Seated next to her was the well-to-do gentleman wearing the emerald and the French-tailored suit. Shell wondered briefly if they were traveling together, then decided they weren't when the girl caught him looking at her and gave him a lewd smile and a wink. She was available if he was. Embarrassed by her boldness, Shell averted his gaze.

Beneath him, he could hear the wheels of the stage breaking through the frozen snow with a gritty crunch. It was a calm, cloudy Colorado morning, and Shell kept his hands buried deep within the pockets of his mackinaw. The passenger next to him, a hard-rock miner with a pale face and watery eyes, sneezed violently several times and blew his nose. The red-haired girl made a face.

In one way, Shell couldn't believe he was doing this. In another way, he felt as if he had never done anything else. He was backsliding into something he thought he had given up for good.

Three successful holdups were behind him—one train and two coaches—and if all went well, today's heist would make the fourth. Each of the robberies he and Vic, Joe Finney, and Darby James had pulled off had been different from the first, never displaying any set pattern that might give the law something to work on and use against them. Wells Fargo agents and peace officers alike had their hackles up, but their search for "Vic Taylor and his band of hoodlums," as one newspaper had put it, had been unsuccessful thus far.

This was Shell's first inside job, and the first time he was unable to mask his identity. He had made up for the lack of concealment by wearing a hat and growing a mustache and a short-clipped beard. With his collar up and his hat brim pulled low, no one at the Burkville stage station had recognized him. This was no small feat, considering his own reward dodger had been tacked to the wall directly behind the agent's head. Shell had spotted the poster when he bought his ticket, and while he managed to keep a tight grip on his nerves, he almost tripped over his own feet in his haste to get out of there and board the stage.

He thought about the job at hand. Twenty rugged miles separated the mining center of Burkville from the nearest train depot in Dillon, and gold shipments, mail, and passengers, in that order of importance, were transported over this route whenever the weather and traveling conditions allowed. How much gold might be in the green Wells Fargo chest in the front boot of the stagecoach, Shell didn't know, but there were two shotgun guards, one sitting in the seat beside the driver and another riding horseback fifty yards to their rear, and that told him something about this particular shipment; it wasn't going to make them all rich, but it would be enough of a pay-off to compensate them for their troubles.

It had been Shell's business to determine whether or not there would be a shipment to leave Burkville today and send word back to Vic, and it was while he was loitering around the station that he singled out the gentleman now seated across from him. Having already looked him over with a practiced eye, Shell concluded that this man could afford to share the wealth, too.

Shell's gaze wandered back to where the emerald was glittering beneath the fleshy double chin and settled there. It looked real. It might be worth enough money to keep Sally comfortable in Denver throughout the winter. It might make her smile again. He hadn't seen her in almost three months, and they hadn't parted company on pleasant terms.

He was suddenly aware that the gentleman had lifted a hand to touch the emerald at his throat and was watching him intently. Shell realized he had been staring at the gem too steadily, showing too much interest, something he never would have done had he kept his mind on business instead of personal problems.

Without acting flustered or evasive, he calmly met the older man's gaze and smiled.

The man returned his smile, politely enough, and let his gloved hand drop back down to rest on his knee. "Do you like it?"

Shell nodded. "Looks expensive."

"It is. My wife, bless her heart, purchased it from one of

New York City's top jewelers and gave it to me for our anniversary."

For lack of anything better to say, Shell used his favorite expression and added a touch of wonderment to his voice.

"Is that right?"

"Certainly. She picked it out herself."

"Your wife's got good taste."

"In jewelry or men?" The gentleman laughed at his own witty remark and leaned toward Shell, extending his hand. "I'm Bayard Wallace. Perhaps you've heard of me."

"No, sir. Afraid I haven't had the pleasure."

They shook hands, a single, hard pump.

Bayard Wallace looked a trifle perturbed. "Then you must not read the papers," he said. "I dare say there isn't a Colorado newspaper in existence that hasn't mentioned my name on the front page at least a dozen times within the last ten years."

"Is that . . ." Shell stopped himself. "Really?"

"I have mining interests all over this fine state," Wallace told him. "It's a right healthy industry to invest in if you have the know-how and the capital."

"I don't know a whole lot about mining," Shell confessed.

Wallace laughed. "Nonsense, young man. Anyone who has ever spent a gold or silver coin knows a great deal about mining. Money and mining go hand in hand, you see."

The man next to Shell snorted in disgust. "Unless you're a miner," he said.

The girl with the red hair giggled, and the three men fell silent. Bayard Wallace's face flushed slightly. Shell figured he didn't know as much about mining as he thought he did.

Nudging the girl's flowery travel case aside with his toe, Shell propped both feet on the middle bench and tried to make himself as comfortable as he could despite the rickety, rackety pounding of the stage. This was a hell of way to get from one place to another. Shell thought he would rather have walked.

Resting his head against the back of the seat, he drew a deep breath and immediately wished he hadn't. He felt his throat constrict, blocking the air to his lungs, and his feet slid off the bench in a hurry as he sat up.

Elbows on knees, head in his hands, Shell spent the next two minutes waging his own silent battle against the maddening tickle inside his throat. He needed desperately to cough but couldn't for lack of air, and even if he managed to catch his breath, it was liable to trigger a gut-wrenching coughing spell. Swallowing hard over and over, he struggled to squeeze a little air at a time into his lungs and felt his body break out in a sweat. He had the wild urge to tear off his coat, buttons and all, but was afraid to move.

Ever so slowly, his erratic breathing evened out some. He felt weak and shaky and was aware that he was wheezing. He swiped at his watering eyes. This was his first spell of the winter, and he knew it wouldn't be the last, nor the worst.

"Honey, you all right?"

He glanced up at the redhead, who had been watching him and cleared his throat before speaking. "Yeah, I'm fine."

"You look sick to me."

"It's nothing."

Her heavily powdered face puckered a little in a frown. "So long as it's not contagious. Is it?"

He shook his head.

"Good." The frown vanished. "You wanna trade places with Mr. Wallace and lay your head in my lap? I don't mind."

Shell managed a smile. "That's all right. Thanks anyway."

"You change your mind, sweetie, just say so."

Feeling like a fool, Shell tried to ignore her. He was glad

Sally wasn't here to see this. Sweetie. She would have teased him unmercifully over that one.

His hands still trembling, Shell unbuttoned his mackinaw and felt the sweat on his chest and stomach turn to ice. He quickly buttoned up again. A doctor had told him several years ago he'd probably die of pneumonia someday, but he saw no sense in accelerating the process.

"Why are we slowing down?" the girl asked suddenly.

Everyone looked at her, then at one another. Shell's mouth went dry, and a powerful rush of adrenaline left him feeling almost giddy.

The coach was slowing, moving at a snail's pace now, and he heard the driver and shotgun guard exchange words in low, urgent voices as they pulled to a stop. Tying up the leather curtain on the window next to him, Shell took one swift look outside, spotted Joe Finney running toward them across the frozen snow, and drew his Colt.

The driver or guard one, he wasn't sure which, spoke loud enough for the passengers to hear him inside the coach. "Everybody stay seated and do whatever they tell you. Don't try any heroics."

"You heard the man." Shell spoke quietly and raised his gun. "No heroics."

The miner, the financier, and the prostitute stared at him in stunned disbelief. Shell lifted the miner's sidearm from its worn holster and tossed it out the window, then motioned for him to sit between Bayard Wallace and the girl. Scowling at him, the miner did as he was told. Outside, Vic ordered the driver to throw down the strongbox, and his tone of voice was all business. Darby James had ridden up with the second guard in tow and was holding a shotgun on him.

"Y'all keep your hands where I can see them and stay calm," Shell said, and his cool gaze rested upon Bayard

Wallace. "The pin. Hand it over."

The man's face seemed to swell. "I'll be damned if I will!"

Shell cocked his gun. "Mr. Wallace, you'll be damned if you don't," he said evenly. "I want the pin, your pocket watch, and your wallet. Right now."

Shell Paxton's composure, his lack of emotion, was as convincing as the cocked six-shooter. Bayard Wallace obeyed without another word, laying his worldly possessions on the bench in front of Shell.

"You have a money belt?"

Wallace glared at him, not answering.

Shell glanced outside in time to see Vic break the lock on the treasure chest, then looked back at Bayard Wallace. "I'll find out one way or another," he said.

Very slowly, Wallace unbuttoned his suitcoat and vest, his white shirt, and finally his longjohns, and after a moment of huffing and puffing, drew the belt from around his ample waist and handed it over. Shell hid it beneath his coat.

"I got forty-five cents," the miner said, spitting the words. "I guess you want that, too."

Shell's dark, bearded face lit up as he smiled at the out-at-the-pants miner and slipped a twenty-dollar gold piece from his own pocket. "When you get to Dillon," he said and tossed him the double eagle, "buy yourself a hot meal and take it easy."

The man stared at him in astonishment.

Joe Finney poked his head in the window and looked at the three passengers. "They give you any trouble?"

"No. Take care of them, will you?"

"Sure." Joe craned his neck to get a better look at the girl. "I'll feel 'em over, make sure they're unarmed."

Shell kicked the opposite door open and jumped outside. All seemed to be running smoothly and according to plan.

Vic was taking pouches of gold dust from the chest and placing them into a gunny sack, while Darby James kept the driver and guards covered. They were lying on their stomachs in the snow, legs and arms spread wide.

Vic glanced up at Shell as he approached him. "Not a bad haul."

"About how much?"

"Enough to go around," Vic said shortly.

"You about ready to get out of here?"

Vic nodded, then frowned when he heard the girl's shrill voice raised in protest. "Go see what they're up to."

Shell walked around to the other side of the stagecoach, looking around him for the first time. The sun was trying to break through the clouds, and the white-clad mountains glittered beneath its light. Tall pines and spruce, heavy with snow, towered above him and laid their cool, blue shadows across the road.

Shell drew up beside the wheel team and rested a hand on the warm, shaggy rump of the off horse. He saw that Bayard Wallace and the miner were lying on the ground beside the other three men, but no one was watching over them. Half-smiling, Darby was staring toward the coach instead, where Joe Finney and the girl were each struggling to gain possession of her small, green pocketbook. Joe finally snatched it away from her and shoved her against the coach's rear boot. He held the pocketbook above her head and just out of reach of her flailing arms, teasing her with it and laughing as she hopped around him. She stumbled, and he caught hold of the front of her dress, bunching up the material in his fist.

"Now let's see what else we got here."

Hands on her hips, breasts heaving, she didn't try to break free. "Fine! Do what you want. Just give me back my purse!"

"Man, listen to her." Joe glanced at Darby and grinned.

"The little bitch is really begging for it, ain't she?"

"Flip a coin and see who gets to go first," Darby said.

"Maybe we should just take her with us."

"Maybe you should give her the purse and stop screwing around. We've got a job to do."

Both Joe and Darby turned to look at Shell, and their smiles faded and died. Joe pushed the girl roughly aside.

"Texas, you'd better grow another inch or two 'fore you start spoutin' off. Little fellas like you sometimes get stepped on."

Chill, dark eyes appraised him. "It'll take a bigger man than you, Finney," he said softly.

Something in Shell Paxton's expression made Joe back up mentally and take a better look. He licked his lips. No one spoke. The five men on the ground watched the two outlaws in silence while the snow melted beneath their bodies, soaking them to the skin. Eyes wide, teeth chattering, they waited for something to happen.

Darby James spoke up, his voice low. "Joe, if he tries for his gun, I'll cut him in two."

Out of the corner of his eye, Shell saw the boy's shotgun raised and pointed his way. And something else. A flash of movement, one of the guards rising to his hands and knees, swiftly, jumping to his feet.

Taken by surprise, Darby yelled and swung his shotgun like a club as the man rushed him.

What happened afterwards would haunt Shell for a long time to come. Momentarily stunned, the man hit the ground on his side, rolled over, and gazed up at Darby. The boy stood over him with the shotgun, panting and wild-eyed, and cast a quick look at Vic Taylor as he strode toward them. Darby opened his mouth to say something a second before Vic backhanded him across the face and knocked him sprawling. He dropped his shotgun, and the man on the ground scrambled for it, body wriggling across the snow. His hand closed on the stock, but he never got any further. A wet, scuffed-up boot came down, pinning the shotgun to the ground, and when the guard continued to tug on the gunstock, Vic Taylor calmly drew his .45, waited for the man to look up, and shot him between the eyes.

Brain matter and pieces of bone exploded out the back of his skull.

Screaming, the girl cringed against the side of the coach and pressed a trembling hand to her mouth. Darby James vomited, heaved, vomited again. The color drained from Shell's face.

Seemingly unconscious of the man twitching at his feet, Vic looked from Darby to Joe. "The next one of you that fouls up gets the same. Understood?"

Dumbstruck, neither said a word. Vic replaced the spent cartridge in his gun, holstered it, and stepped over the dead man's body. He flung a hard look in Shell's direction.

"Well, don't just stand there with your thumb up your ass. Go get the horses."

CHAPTER NINE

"I'll see your raise and bump it ten."

More matchsticks joined the growing pile in the center of the table, a second round of cards were dealt, and three solemn sets of eyes flicked from the cards lying face-up on the table to the hole cards hidden away within cupped palms.

"King's high. Your bet, Vic."

Sally Paxton mixed up four cocktails, a trick she had learned during her stint at the Silver Buckle, and carried them to the table by the stove where Shell, Vic, and Leo Moffat were engrossed in a game of five-card stud. They were supposed to be having fun, playing for matches instead of money to keep things friendly, but she sensed an underlying tension here that contrasted greatly with the laughter and guitar music coming from across the room. Serving the drinks, she glanced at the men lounging at the bar and caught Joe Finney's eye on her. Sally had seen that look before. Ignoring his brazen stare, she sat close to Shell and watched the game.

Outside, a blizzard was blowing hard and furious, hurling snow and ice against the windows, but Leo Moffat's saloon was cozily warm. Leo did very little business during these harsh winter months so they had the place to themselves. Vic, Joe, Darby, Shell—they were all here, along with six other men Sally had never met, more of Leo's comrades—everybody enjoying one another's company, the whiskey, and the warmth. Sally wished she could say the same.

When Shell sent word to her in Denver to meet him here, she had wasted no time in making the trip. Since her arrival at noon, however, they hadn't had a single moment of privacy, and she was beginning to wonder if they ever would.

Vic Taylor counted out several matches and tossed them into the pile. "Twenty."

Teeth clamped on a smelly cigar, Leo took another look at his hole cards and folded. "Damned good thing we're not playing for money tonight," he grumbled.

Vic grinned at Shell. "How about it, kid? You in or out?"

Sally knew Vic was bluffing. The only time he smiled during a poker game was when he was holding lousy cards and wanted everyone to think the opposite. She had also discovered that he was a sore loser. Matches or no, he played to win and grew sour and short of temper when he didn't.

Shell's hand was a good one, the best he'd had all night, yet he hesitated, and Sally couldn't believe it when he dropped his cards face-down on the table, deliberately losing so that Vic could win. Furious, she kicked him in the shin and saw him wince.

She might have understood the bluff had it been part of Shell's strategy, but this made the fourth time in the past hour he had folded a winning hand when directly confronted by Vic. What was the matter with him anyway?

Still angry and wanting Shell to notice it, Sally glared at him, watched him slowly sip his drink, shuffle the cards, and deal. He was doing a fine job of ignoring her, and she had an urge to kick him again but didn't. Strange as he was acting, it wouldn't have surprised her if he kicked back.

Sally hadn't seen Shell in three very long months, making the change she saw in him tonight more obvious. He seemed on edge, tensed up, certainly not his usual relaxed self, and it was the most noticeable when he was around Vic. It brought to mind something Sally had suspected ever since she had known him. She had a feeling he was afraid of Vic Taylor.

"Shell tells me you're quite a poker player," Vic said abruptly. He was looking at her, lolling a piece of candy around in his mouth. "Sure you don't want to sit in with us?"

She smiled coolly at him and ran a finger around the brim of her goblet. "Not tonight."

"Suit yourself." He turned his attention back to Shell. "Last card, kid. Make it a good one."

Sally frowned, irritated by Vic's pet name for her husband. Besides the more well-known definitions of the word, kid was also the slang term for a child pickpocket, and Sally disliked the connotation.

Leo suddenly slammed his cards down on the table and squirmed around in his chair to look back at the eight men at the bar. Darby James was strumming an old beat-up guitar, playing the same monotonous tune over and over, while Joe and another man sang, their semi-drunk voices wandering off on different keys.

"Hey! Shut the bloody hell up, will you?"

The music came to an abrupt end as the guitarist and singers looked at Leo in surprise.

Vic shook his head. "You boys couldn't carry a tune in a corked jug. Now Shell here, he's a different story." Vic smiled at him. "Why don't you play something, show 'em how it's done."

"That's a good idea," Leo said, brightening. "It's been a long time since I've heard you play and sing, Shell."

Shell appeared uncomfortable. "You haven't missed nothing." Sally saw his jaws clench.

"Ah, come on," Vic urged. "Darby, bring the guitar."

"Vic, it's been a long time. I'm out of practice."

Leo slapped him on the back. "You'll do fine," he said and turned to Sally. "Shell used to play here sometimes. He tell you that?"

Sally was surprised. "No, he didn't."

"Drew quite a crowd. Great for business."

Looking at Shell, Sally thought of his guitar they had left behind in Texas. He had played it at night when he wasn't too tired, mostly during the winter when there was less work to do, but rarely had she heard him sing. The fact that he had done both before a crowd shocked her. There was still so much about this quiet, private man she had yet to discover.

Idly thumbing the deck of cards, Shell watched Darby walk over and hold the guitar out to him. He accepted it reluctantly and glanced at Sally. She smiled her encouragement, looking forward to hearing him as much as Leo and Vic.

"Sing that song you made up. The slow, pretty one," Leo said.

Leaning back, one foot resting on the rung of Sally's chair, Shell struck a few running chords. The men gathered around, quiet and waiting. He tightened a string, strummed a few more chords, and seemed to relax as his fingers warmed to their task. Calloused, brown hands coaxed more sound out of Darby's old guitar than anyone ever had. He began to sing, very softly at first, dark eyes focused on some distant object, singing more to himself than to the people around him. He sang as effortlessly as he played, the music flowing, sad, and slow. Outside, the blizzard raged on, but no one heard it.

Entranced, Sally listened to the poetic cadence of his words, surprised that a man who had never learned to read or write could compose lines as expressive as these. It was a song of loneliness. It was Shell's song, and she was sorry when it ended.

The room was deathly still. Shell glanced around at them.

"Like I said, it's been a long time."

"That was pretty. Real pretty," Leo said in a quiet voice.

"Sing another one."

"Do you know 'Lorena?' " someone asked.

"Some of it. I'll see what I can do."

After two sad songs in a row, he lifted their sagging spirits with "Buffalo Gals" and a couple of lively Spanish-sounding tunes he'd picked up in Mexico. He sang "Dixie" for Vic who had served in the Confederacy, and those who knew the words joined in. He played another song then that none of them had ever heard, and Sally wondered if this, too, was his own. The lyrics were spellbinding, and when he laid down the guitar at last, no one spoke or made a sound.

A fleeting smile crossed Darby James' face. "Guess I need to practice a little more," he said finally.

The spell broken, everyone laughed.

Leo watched the men slowly gravitate back toward the bar. "You've got real talent," he said to Shell.

Sally agreed. He had made them feel the music, and for a short while, she had forgotten everything else.

Shell seemed more at ease now, but whether it was the music that had done the trick or the cocktails, Sally didn't know. She watched him talk, laugh, and drink with Leo and Vic and tried as discreetly as possible to fan some of Leo's cigar smoke from her face. She needed to get out of here. She needed fresh air.

Reaching beneath the table, her fingers closed on Shell's thigh, and she squeezed, hard. When he looked at her, she smiled at Vic and Leo, excused herself, and casually walked into the game room where it was cooler. She found and lit the lamp by the door and looked around her at the baize-covered card tables. There were keno and faro layouts along the opposite wall, and next to her was a pool table. Reaching down, she picked up the eight ball and idly flipped it from one hand to the other while she waited.

It was only a moment before the door opened and closed behind her, and she turned to see Shell. Neither said a word as he drew her into his arms.

Bodies pressed close, he kissed her mouth, face, and neck, whiskey-hot breath tickling her, hands caressing her, sliding down to her hips. His touch sent shivers up and down Sally's back, and she giggled in spite of herself.

"God, I missed you."

The emotion in his voice surprised her. Tipping her head back slightly, she studied him. Unshaven, he appeared older, more like his twenty-eight years. His hair was growing too long. Smiling a little, Sally brushed it off his forehead and out of his eyes.

"Let's go upstairs," he whispered. "Be alone . . ."

She shook her head, more serious now. "We need to talk."

"Later."

"No, now. This is important, Shell."

"It can't wait?"

"No." She stared gravely into his eyes. "I'm sick and tired of these long separations."

He touched her face, tracing the curve of her cheek with a forefinger. "So am I."

"It's like we're not even married anymore," she said. "You just don't have any idea how lonely it gets."

Shell smiled. "I think I do." He backed her into a corner of the room and placed his hands against the wall on either side of her head. "It won't be like this forever. Think you can stick it out a little while longer?"

"I don't know. I'm scared something's gonna happen to you before that time finally rolls around. Shell, I want us to be together again, working together, like we used to. I want a real family again." A troubled frown shadowed her face. "I feel so empty. After Laurie died . . ."

"Sally, do we have to talk about that now?"

"After Laurie died," she continued, relentless, "I wanted a baby more than ever. Is that so much to ask? Why is it other people can have a whole houseful of children, and you and me can't even have one?"

He sighed wearily. "I don't know."

"I don't either. All I know is that it's hard enough as it is without you being gone all the time. I thought you wanted to settle down and raise a family."

"I do."

"Then tell me something. How are we supposed to accomplish this if you're never around? We don't even have a place to live."

"Baby, we've got more than a place to live. We've got money, more than we've ever had, and there's more on the way." He chucked her on the chin and smiled. "I want to give our kids the things I never got."

"They'd have parents who love them. Isn't that enough?"

He shook his head. "You can't buy anything with love. I want them to get a good education, Sally. And whatever else they want."

"You'd spoil them rotten with stolen money. Don't you feel even a little guilty? After we were married, you never took anything from anybody if it wasn't yours."

Shell's face clouded. "And you think because I lived like a saint for six years that I wasn't tempted as hell?"

"Were you?" Sally asked, unable to keep the surprise out of her voice.

She watched him move away from her and gaze out the frosty window. "It's sort of like an addiction, I guess," he said after a moment.

"But you never gave in to it until you went to see Vic," Sally pointed out. "You're a good and decent man, Shell, through and through. With the money we've saved up, you could leave Vic now and start over in Arizona just like we planned."

He looked at her. "No, I've gone too far to back out now, and besides . . ." he lowered his voice, ". . . things aren't as simple as they were."

"What are you talking about?"

He turned back toward the window, and she sensed again his uneasiness.

"Two weeks ago," he said quietly, "Vic killed a man, a Wells Fargo guard." The words were strained, as if he still couldn't quite believe it. "It's not just robbery anymore," he went on. "It's murder."

"Oh, no." Sally sat down, hands clasped tightly in her lap. She stared at her husband's back. "What happened, Shell? Why did he do it?"

He shook his head. "I don't know. He just killed him . . . in cold blood. No reason for it. No reason at all." He paused a long time and when he finally turned to look at her, a pained expression still lingered in his eyes. "He pulled the trigger, but we were all in on it."

"All the more reason for you to leave him as soon as possible," Sally said desperately.

Shell frowned. "I can't. We made a deal, and if that gold bullion is really there in New Mexico, we're gonna need it. Especially now. We'll leave the country. We'll . . ."

"Is that why you're doing this?" Sally broke in. "For the money? Or is it because you're afraid?"

"Afraid of what?"

"Of Vic."

Eyes narrowing slightly, he watched her, saying nothing.

"That's it, isn't it?" she said. "You're afraid of him. You always have been, I think."

"Stop talking crazy."

"I'm not, and you darned well know it," she snapped. "He's got you under his thumb. Not only that, but he's a jealous old man, Shell."

"Jealous? What are you talking about?"

"Jealous of you and me. Vic's attitude toward you changed the minute you married me. Can't you see the difference in him? Sometimes he acts almost as if he despises you."

"He was just upset because I left his gang," Shell argued. "And for good reason, I guess. I'm obligated to him."

"No, you're not."

"Vic's done a lot for me over the years."

"By using you and turning you into an outlaw?"

He shook his head. "That was my doing. Not his. I could've got out anytime."

"You were twelve years old, Shell!"

"Old enough to know right from wrong."

Sally was at a loss. There was no getting through to him. Vic Taylor had murdered a man in cold blood no more than two weeks ago, yet Shell was standing here defending him. It was unbelievable. Vic really had him hoodwinked.

Shell lifted her to her feet and held her close. "Sally, try to understand," he said. "I'm doing this for us. Come spring, soon as it warms up, we're going to New Mexico for that gold. We may or may not find it, but either way I gotta know you're behind me."

Sally shook her head, refusing to accept another one of Vic Taylor's get-rich schemes. It still amazed her that someone as practical-minded as Shell could fall for something so out-landish. She told him as much.

"Come on, Sally. Don't be that way. Vic said . . ."

He let his voice trail off when he heard Vic calling him for another game of cards. They both looked toward the door, then at each other.

Sally's left eyebrow arched. "Well?"

"Well what?"

"Is it me or him?"

Vic yelled again, telling him to hurry up. He sounded drunk.

Shell swore softly, whispering it, and looked back down at her. "One more game," he said. "A short one, then we'll go up to our room and not come down for two days. How does that sound?"

She pulled away from him. "Oh, it sounds fine and dandy. Be sure and invite Vic. He can sleep in the middle!"

She turned her back on him and left. On her way out the door, she shot Vic a seething look, bunched her skirts up in front, and stomped upstairs, creating a scene and too mad to care.

CHAPTER TEN

North Central New Mexico: May, 1889

The place stank of billy goats. Goats, damp wood, spring-time . . . and a faint stench Shell couldn't quite place.

He was sitting relaxed astride his black, snip-nosed mare, looking around him at what was left of the town of Last Chance. There was little to see. When Adam Chaney's mine played out, stores and houses were torn apart board by board and hauled to the next boom town where they were nailed to-gether again. Only that which could not be moved or was use-less had been left behind.

Shell supposed it was a fitting place for the one-time bandit, Malo Chavez, to make his home. Among the crum-bling stone buildings, weeds, and heaps of bottles and rusty cans, Chavez talked to his goats and chickens and dreamed of eight golden ingots and the angry spirits of the dead who watched over them.

But Shell didn't see Chavez . . . or his goats. The town, the whole valley in fact, was silent, vacant.

Vic dismounted in front of the square, flat-roofed building that had once served as the assay office where Chavez now lived. Despite the early morning chill, there was no woodsmoke curling from the chimney as one would have ex-pected. Vic called out to Chavez several times, and when no one answered, he pushed the door open and stepped inside. Shell saw him raise a hand to his nose but didn't think any-thing of it until he left his horse and walked toward the house. When he neared the open door, the high, powerful stench of rotting flesh drove him backwards with such force it was as if he had been physically shoved.

Malo Chavez was dead and had been for several days.

Pressing his bandana to his mouth and nose, Shell peered inside. Chavez was propped in a kitchen chair so that he faced the door and might have appeared very natural and lifelike before his body became so grossly bloated. Whoever had killed him had crossed his legs, tucked a corncob pipe into the corner of his mouth, and had placed his battered sombrero on his head at a jaunty angle. But for the blood stains on the front of his shirt, anyone would have thought Malo Chavez had sat down to enjoy his pipe and simply forgot to inhale.

The dead man's hands were clasped together in his lap and between the swollen fingers was a slip of paper. Vic snatched it free and joined Shell outside.

Holding the note gingerly between his thumb and forefinger, he glanced at Shell and grinned. "Life's just chock full of surprises, ain't it?"

Shell swallowed hard a couple of times, having trouble keeping his breakfast down, and made no comment. He'd had enough surprises in the past few months to last him a lifetime.

Vic read the note, passed it to Shell, and looked around him at the town and the surrounding mountains with narrowed eyes. "Adam Chaney," he mumbled.

"You think he's the one killed Chavez?"

"Who else?"

Shell looked at the note. Five words. He tried to sound out the letters one by one, couldn't make sense of it, and gave up. "What does it say?"

"Says, 'Dead men don't need gold.' " Vic shook his head. "At least he's got a sense of humor. And he knew we were coming. Malo must have told him about us."

"Why would he kill him?"

"Why does Chaney do anything? Crazy bastard. He's trying to scare us off."

"At least he's got a reason," Shell murmured.

"What?"

Accusation lurking in his eyes, Shell looked at him. One corner of his mouth twitched slightly. "I said, at least Chaney had a reason for killing him." He shrugged and looked away, his gaze sweeping aimlessly over the ghost town. "What now?"

"Exactly what we set out to do," Vic said. He gave Shell a sharp, probing look before mounting up. "That is, if you think you're up to it."

"Why wouldn't I be?"

Gazing down at him, Vic leaned forward in the saddle and rested an arm on the pommel. "You look sickly," he said. "Joe thinks you're consumptive."

"You know I'm not."

"I know, but Joe and Darby don't." He straightened in the saddle. "You'd better perk up. If we find that gold, I won't have time to play nursemaid."

Shell's fists clenched. "You won't have to."

Vic nodded and reined his horse around as if to leave.

"What about Chavez?" Shell called out. "You're not gonna just leave him to rot, are you?" Vic glanced over his shoulder at him. "Smells to me like he's well on his way already. Of course, if you want to bury him, be my guest."

"He was your friend. Not mine."

Vic didn't appear to have heard him.

Shell looked back toward the shack. He didn't think he could stomach it. He swung into the saddle and followed Vic out of town in a westerly direction to where they had made camp the night before. They had left Joe and Darby early this morning to care for the mules and pack up while they paid Malo Chavez a final visit before beginning their search. He guessed Vic was probably glad the old man was dead. He had never liked the idea of sharing the gold with him anyway.

Thinking of Chavez and Adam Chaney, Shell half-expected a bullet to lodge between his shoulder blades. He looked toward the nearest piñon-covered slope. Chaney would be keeping a sharp eye on them. Maybe he was watching them right this minute, hiding up there in those trees with a good long-range rifle and an unstable mentality to accompany it. The hairs on the back of Shell's neck stiffened. He spoke softly to his horse and hurried to catch up with Vic.

The sun was peeking at them over the tops of the pines. Its warming rays touched Shell's back and turned the mare's coat a glistening blue-black. All around them, new grass and leaves and wildflowers sparkled with dew. The snow had melted on all but the higher reaches of the Sangre de Cristo Range, and Shell was glad to see the last of it.

He felt wrung out. Winters always dealt him a severe physical blow, but this one had been particularly hard, and even now, the brassy taste of blood still lingered on his tongue from this morning's bout of coughing, and his lungs ached with each breath. Reaching back, he dug a full bottle of whiskey from the saddlebag and washed out his mouth, leaning to the side to spit, swallowing only enough to clear his throat. Straight whiskey was becoming an acquired taste with him, one of those habits he'd rather do without but found he couldn't.

Vic gave him a sidelong look and grinned. "Better keep that hid. Joe'll have it drunk up 'fore a cat can lick its ass."

Shell nodded, tucked the bottle deep into his saddlebag, and buckled the flap.

Looking uncomfortable, Vic watched him, frowning slightly. "Listen, kid, I'm sorry if I was a little hard on you earlier. Guess I got a funny way of showing it, but I'm obliged to you for throwing in with me. You're my right-hand man, you know. Always have been."

Riding next to him, Shell looked straight ahead, keeping his eyes on the space between his horse's ears, saying nothing.

Vic shrugged. "These one-sided conversations are gettin' pretty old," he remarked. "You're still riled because I killed that guard. All right, so let's talk about it." When Shell still made no comment, he continued. "Anyone'd think you'd never seen me kill a man before."

"I haven't. Not in cold blood."

"How many times do I have to tell you he asked for it?" Vic demanded. "He gambled and lost. Hell, kid, life's cheap." He suddenly burst out laughing. "And you have to admit Joe and Darby are almighty well-behaved lately."

Shell's mouth tightened. They had discussed this twice already, and he had yet to find anything funny about it.

Ninety-nine percent of the heists Shell had taken part in with Vic Taylor had been pulled off with timed precision. You got the upper hand, you stayed calm and in command, you took what you wanted, and you left. That wasn't to say they had never been forced to shoot their way out of a tight situation, but these instances were rare, and no one on either side had been seriously hurt. Now, with the brutal murder of the guard tainting their names, rewards for their capture had more than doubled, and every law officer and tin-pot bounty hunter in the country was on the lookout for them. Worse than that, Vic didn't even care.

Ahead of him, Shell could see Joe and Darby mounted up and ready. The four pack mules were tied nose-to-tail behind Darby's horse.

"Looks like we'll get an early start this morning," he said mildly, changing the subject.

Vic nodded. "Yeah, looks that way." His voice hardened. "You keep one thing in mind. We're in this together. Got it?"

"I wouldn't be here if I didn't."

"You'd better believe it."

The route the four gold seekers took paralleled with the icy runoff waters of the Rio Colorado, winding between sheer rock bluffs and fresh smelling pines, and the sounds of their passing were muffled by the rushing water. Shell felt hemmed in. Like an Indian, he preferred traveling on higher ground where he could see more of the surrounding countryside. He gazed up at the high cliffs above him. Someone with a rifle could pick them off one by one without straining more than his trigger finger.

But no one else appeared worried. Vic was in the lead, followed closely by Joe Finney, Darby James, and the string of mules. Shell brought up the rear, riding several yards behind the others. He could hear Joe and Darby having another one of their endless arguments, swapping insults back and forth in a good-natured fashion. Darby had been trying to convince Joe for the last two days that he was related to the late Jesse James. Second cousins, he claimed. No one believed him.

"You ask anybody in Clay County, Missouri," Darby said. "They'll tell you it's so."

Joe shook his head. "You're full of it, Darb." He grinned. "You probably don't even know who your old man was, much less the rest of your family."

"Hey, Joe? Kiss my lily-white ass."

Shell dropped farther behind them, tired of their constant bickering. It was also a preventive measure. Joe Finney was the type of person who could take one look at somebody and decide then and there if he liked him or not. He hadn't liked

Shell from the start and reminded him of the fact at least a dozen times a day, usually dragging Darby in on it, too. Not in the mood for their snide remarks, Shell kept his distance from them.

The rock bluffs had given way to steep mountain slopes, aspen, and towering spruce. Shell felt his heart hammering against his chest and his breath grow shallow and knew they were gradually climbing higher and higher. Patches of snow still survived within the deeper shadows.

The animals they had chosen for this trip were mountain-bred and sure of foot, and Shell's mare, Snip, was the best of the lot. Small, quick, and eager, she fought the bit, wanting to catch up with the other horses. Shell held her back and finally reined in altogether, his eyes scanning the slope on the other side of the river.

For the past half hour or so, he had had the ominous feeling that someone or something was up there. It was similar to the feeling he got when someone would walk soundlessly into the same room with him; maybe he didn't see or hear them, yet he instinctively knew they were there.

They were standing in the sun, and steam rose from Snip's body. Shell was sweating in his heavy woolen coat. Holding the reins between his teeth, he took it off, rolled it up, and was about to tuck it behind the saddle with his bedroll when he saw a silver glint out of the corner of his eye. His fingers froze as he looked back up at the slope. Something up there had caught the sunlight. Something. A gun barrel perhaps?

He reined his horse within the cover of the trees, still staring toward the place where he had seen the flash of sunlight on steel, but there was nothing now. Skirting the worst of the deadfall and tumbled rocks around the river, he followed the tracks of the horsemen ahead of him.

They had halted some distance down river, waiting for

him while they gave the horses and mules a breather.

Joe Finney hooked a leg around the saddlehorn and watched him ride up. His hat was off, and tiny droplets of sweat had formed on his bald spot. "Well, well, well, Texas. Nice of you to join us."

Shell ignored him and addressed Vic. "There's someone up there." He nodded toward the mountains across from them.

Vic frowned. "Following us, you mean?"

"Could be."

Joe Finney flipped his cigarette into the water and squinted at Shell through the twin streamers of smoke trickling from his nostrils. "How do you know?" he asked.

"I saw something that looked like a rifle barrel catching the light."

"I never saw a thing."

"No, I don't guess you did," Shell admitted, then added more slowly, "If you'd use your eyes more and your mouth less, you might see something sometimes."

Darby laughed out loud, looking from his partner to Shell and back again. Vic barely suppressed a grin.

Joe's long face reddened with anger as he slapped on his hat, but whatever he was about to say was interrupted by Vic.

"If anybody's on our backtrail, it's Adam Chaney," he said and gazed through the trees at the surrounding mountains. "Likely, he'll follow us, hoping we'll lead him to his gold. After we find the gold . . . Well, that's when you can start worrying. Not now."

"Maybe Chaney's not that logical."

"Tex, if you're scared, then turn back," Joe sneered. "It'll leave more money for the rest of us."

"You'd like that, wouldn't you?" Shell said. He was having to work extra hard lately to keep his temper in check.

He turned back to Vic. "Let's get out of this hole where we can see something."

Vic shook his head. "I'll stick to the trail. If you boys want to play it safe and move to higher ground, go ahead."

He spoke to his horse and continued on down the river, picking his way through flood-blasted trees and rocks and whistling a tune through his teeth.

"Better start climbing, Tex." Joe flapped his arms and clucked like a chicken. His horse shied violently and took off, nearly knocking him from the saddle, and Shell heard him laugh as he regained his seat and joined Darby and Vic.

An outsider, Shell followed at a distance and wished he'd kept his mouth shut. He didn't consider himself a coward, but by the same token, he didn't care to end up like Malo Chavez either.

Shell had never taken life for granted. Since childhood, he had clung to it, treasured it, even while his own bad health and a couple of narrow escapes from the law had threatened to steal it away. Besides Sally, it was one of the main reasons why he had left Vic Taylor the first time and the same reason he was determined to break off the partnership again.

Even if they never found the gold hidden in Devil's Canyon, he was through. This time, for good.

Shell had just looked up from the fresh tracks in front of him when a bullet zipped past his head, followed closely by the sound of the shot, and he bailed out of the saddle in the same split second. Gun drawn, eyes wide, he calmed the mare in soft whispers even as he used her body for a shield. She wasn't the only one who was spooked. He scanned the trees, then heard something off to his left and spun around, his Colt cocked and ready.

It was Joe Finney. He led his horse around an outcropping of boulders, and Shell watched in disbelief as he lifted his revolver and pretended to blow the smoke from the barrel.

"You move pretty fast, Tex. Never realized you were so quick on your feet."

"Son of a bitch!" Shell gasped, his nerves still jumping. "What the hell's the matter with you?"

"Just checkin' out my new gun. Not bad, eh?"

"You miss on purpose, or are you a little off your mark today?"

Joe grinned. "I guess you'll never know that for sure, will you?"

Shell's finger tightened on the trigger ever so slightly as Joe drew closer. "I won't miss," he said in a low voice.

Holstering his own gun, Joe Finney stepped into the saddle and looked down at him. "I'm out minding my own business, hunting fresh meat, and you come along and bushwhack me. Now would that be neighborly?"

"Depends on who you ask."

Joe leaned toward him, ignoring the gun pointed in his face. His gray eyes were flat and cold. "Next time you sass me, I may decide to go hunting again and mistake you for wild game. An innocent mistake." He straightened up in the saddle. "It could happen to anybody, Paxton. Even you."

He jerked his mount's head around with the reins and rode off, confident that Shell wouldn't shoot him in the back. He would never know how close he came to getting killed.

CHAPTER ELEVEN

Shell woke up drenched in sweat, visions of a nightmare still flashing before his eyes with frightening clarity. Sometime during the dream, his left hand had closed on a chunk of firewood, mistaking it for a gun, and his knuckles ached from gripping it so long and hard. Working the tightness from his hand, he sat up. His hair was dripping wet, and cold fingers of sweat ran down his back, leaving him chilled.

Rocking back and forth slightly, Shell bunched his blankets around him and stared into the dying embers of the campfire. He waited for the demons to leave his mind.

The same dream had tormented him off and on for months, a recurrent nightmare in which he saw again the Wells Fargo shotgun guard lying on his stomach in the snow, head tilted back, gazing up at Vic Taylor. The guard's features were indistinct, shadowy. All Shell remembered of him were his eyes, the whites of his eyes, as white as the snow, widening in horror as Vic squeezed the trigger.

The shot sounded loud in Shell's ears as the guard's head jerked backwards with the impact, and suddenly there was just the snow, cold and wet beneath Shell's body, and he looked up and saw Vic standing over him. Terrified, knowing in his heart that the man meant to kill him, Shell grabbed for his gun and lifted the muzzle, but his finger kept slipping off the trigger. He tried again and again, frantically, hearing Vic's laughter, but he couldn't keep his finger on the trigger. It was at this point that he usually awoke.

The dream probably lasted no more than a few minutes, but to Shell it seemed endless and was so real he always had trouble meeting Vic's gaze the next morning, afraid the man would see the distrust in his eyes and somehow guess why it was there.

Rousing himself, Shell fed more wood into the fire and listened to Joe snore. Across from him, Vic stirred, looked at him, and immediately rolled over again and was still.

Shell got stiffly to his feet. Dawn was a couple of hours away, and Darby should have come in from his watch by now to start breakfast. Out of the four men, Darby James was the only one who could stir up anything suitable for human consumption, and much to his chagrin, had been elected camp cook.

Putting water on to boil for coffee, Shell wandered out to where the horses were picketed to check on the boy. This would make the third night in a row he had fallen asleep while on watch. When Vic caught him napping that first night, he had belted him across the face and kicked him to his feet. The second time, it was Shell who had found him, and he let the kid sleep. Tonight, he didn't know what he would do. Darby needed another swift kick in the pants, but he didn't care to be the one to do it. No matter how much Shell had been slapped around as a boy, he derived no pleasure out of doing the same to someone else. A disciplinarian he was not.

Snip nickered to him and nibbled at his coat when he drew up beside her. He peered into the darkness beneath the trees. Something, an odd, muffled groan, reached his ears. Nostrils flaring, Snip looked toward the sound, as did Shell, and he wished he'd thought to bring his gun. He called out to Darby in a loud whisper and heard again the same muted sound, only more urgent this time. No longer interested, the black mare blew her warm breath in Shell's face and resumed grazing. Shell stepped away from her, moving cautiously toward a dark form on the ground several yards away that he took to be Darby James. It was.

He was lying on his side, tied and gagged, and Shell could see the whites of his eyes glistening in what little starlight penetrated the dense forest. Casting a wary look around him, Shell dropped to his knees, quickly severed the rope binding Darby's hands and feet, and yanked the gag from his mouth.

"What happened?" he whispered.

Panting, Darby sat up and rubbed his wrists, shaking his head. "Damned if I know." His voice was strained and hoarse. "Caught me off guard. Never had a chance."

"When?"

"Not long ago. Less than half an hour."

Shell looked around him uneasily, then back at Darby. "Who was it? Adam Chaney?"

Still gasping for breath, Darby avoided his gaze, staring into the trees instead and opening and closing his numbed hands.

"Answer me!" Shell hissed. "Did you get a good look at him?"

Darby shook his head. "I was asleep when he jumped me. After he tied me up, he headed towards camp, and all I could see was that he looked pretty big . . . and tall." The boy dragged a hand down his face. "I figured he'd kill all of us."

Relaxing a little, Shell rocked back on his heels and slapped the handle of his knife against his open palm. "He walked towards our camp, huh?"

"Yeah. Then I lost sight of him."

"Didn't say anything to you?"

"Not a word. Just trussed me up, took both my guns, and left."

Shell laughed softly, seeing the full picture now, and Darby looked at him as if he'd lost his mind.

"What the devil are you laughing at?" he demanded. "You

think there's something funny about this?"

"It was Vic."

Darby stared at him. "Huh?"

"I said, it was Vic." Still grinning, Shell glanced over his shoulder in the direction of their camp. "He warned you to keep your eyes open."

"You gotta be kiddin' me."

"I'm not," he said. "Vic did the same thing to me when I was about your age. It's his way of making a point."

Darby swore.

"Scares the hell out of you, doesn't it?"

"The peckerwood," Darby whispered. "He nearly broke my neck. And he's got both my six-shooters."

"Be glad it was Vic and not somebody else."

"Do you think he'll give me back my guns?"

"In his own sweet time."

"He's gonna give 'em to me now," Darby said and started to rise. Shell grabbed his arm and pulled him back down.

"You'd be better off biding your time."

"Why should I? He ain't got the right . . ."

"Makes no difference," Shell broke in. "Your best bet is to act like nothing happened. Don't say a word about it, and you'll get your guns back a lot faster than if you threatened him. Take my word for it."

"I need them now," Darby said miserably.

"Why? Are you figuring to shoot somebody?"

"Maybe." The boy wet his lips, trying to see Shell's expression in the gloom. "If Vic lays a hand on me one more time, I'm liable to do something bad. I'm liable to kill him."

Shell smiled. "Is that a fact?"

"Look here, you think I'm joking?"

"You'd better be."

Darby gazed toward the horses, shaking his head. He

105

seemed to want to talk, seriously for a change, and Shell waited.

"Do you like Vic?" he asked abruptly.

For some reason, his point-blank question caught Shell off guard. No one had ever asked him that before.

When he failed to answer, Darby nodded. "Didn't think so. I tell you what, next time he pushes me around, he's gonna get a bellyful of lead."

"You wouldn't have a chance," Shell said quietly. He stabbed the damp earth with his knife, eyes lowered. "Even if you got lucky and beat him to the draw, he'd live long enough to plant a bullet in your heart."

"I don't know about that. He bleeds like you and me."

Shell glanced up at him and frowned. "Vic's like a big grizzly bear. Unless you hit his brain or his heart with that first shot, you're a dead duck. A bullet anywhere else'll only make him killing mad." He paused, remembering. "One time this fella plugged Vic four times," he said after a moment, his tone of voice resembling that of an awestruck boy. "Man, he was fast. Caught Vic by surprise, but he killed that gunslinger with one shot." He touched a finger to his forehead and looked over at Darby. "Right here."

"You make him sound unkillable."

Shell shrugged. "I'm just saying if you intend to kill him anytime soon, you'd better start working on your aim."

"Yeah, well . . . I'll keep that in mind. Are you gonna tell him what I said?"

"Wasn't planning on it."

Darby smiled. "Thanks. I owe you one."

"Just take my advice and don't brace Vic. He never loses."

The boy thought about that a while and watched the blade of Shell's knife flash as he stabbed at the ground. "You know something?" he said at length. "No matter what Joe says, I think you're all right, most times. But you're a beat dog. Vic's got you so cowed you have to ask his permission to go take a leak. He's not gonna do that to me. I won't stand for it."

Making no comment, Shell gave the ground in front of him one final, vicious stab, got to his feet, and walked back to camp.

Though he wasn't sure why, Shell kept his word and didn't mention Darby James' threats to Vic. Even so, he knew from experience that little got past the big man and had a feeling Vic was well aware that something had occurred behind his back. By noon of that same day, he was sure of it.

They had stopped on the banks of a small lake to rest themselves and the animals and eat a bite when Vic suddenly took off his hat, reached inside, and drew a folded paper from beneath the inner lining. Joe Finney's eager eyes rested on the paper, and he bumped Darby in the ribs to get his attention.

"Is that the map Malo Chavez gave you?" he asked.

"Yep."

"So that's where you kept the damned thing!" he exclaimed, not bothering to hide the fact he had been searching for it. "I knew you didn't throw it away."

Vic ignored his outburst. Unfolding the map, he held it up for Joe, Darby, and Shell to see and struck a match. He looked around at the three of them, half-smiling, and his gaze rested longest on Shell.

"Just so you boys don't get any ideas," he said and calmly touched the flame to a corner of Malo Chavez's map.

Their faces twisted in agony, Joe and Darby watched helplessly as the paper burned. The wind caught the ashes and rolled them across the ground and into the water.

Satisfied, Vic slipped a peppermint into his mouth and

leaned back on his elbows. "Looks like y'all need me more'n you thought you did," he said and gave them a wide grin.

It was then that Shell realized Vic Taylor no longer trusted him.

CHAPTER TWELVE

Former Deputy U.S. Marshal, Bud Thompson, poured a generous measure of water into his whiskey and smiled sheepishly. "Can't stand the stuff straight anymore. Old stomach balls up in a knot."

"Is that why you turned in your badge?" Jesse asked. "Because you couldn't stand the heat?"

Thompson shrugged, bloodshot eyes focused dimly on his glass of watered-down bourbon. "I reckon," he mumbled. "Reflexes are too slow, eyesight's fadin', and I got stomach ulcers. What else could I do?" Squinting, he glanced up at Jesse. "You're what? Forty some-odd years old, right? Mark my words, it'll hit you, too, one of these days. Some fine morning you'll wake up old, and there won't be a damn thing you can do about it."

Jesse Watts frowned, wondering how to shift the conversation back to his own immediate concerns without sounding too abrupt. Bud Thompson was one of the few lawmen he liked, but sitting across from him in this dingy, rat-hole saloon and listening as he recited his many ailments was depressing. It seemed Bud had given up far more than his badge.

"About Vic Taylor . . ." Jesse began.

"Oh, yeah. I apologize, Jess. Sometimes I get to feeling sorry for myself . . ." Bud's voice trailed off. "Where were we now?"

"I was telling you about Vic Taylor and Shell Paxton. I was wondering if you'd heard anything about them since the last time we talked."

Bud nodded and grinned. "They've upped the bounty on both of 'em."

"How much?"

"Paxton's worth two thousand now, and Taylor's worth eight. Seems he killed a shotgun guard a while back."

"I heard about that," Jesse said and paused to light his cigarette. "Any word on Paxton's wife?"

"Yeah, she's right here in Denver, just like you said all along. Been going by the name of Sally Gibson."

Jesse favored his old friend with a rare smile. "How do you do it? I turned this city upside down looking for her."

"Informants. They're the key to my success, Jesse. Anyway, you won't have any use for Sally Paxton when I tell you what else I found out."

"What's that?"

"My source told me Taylor, Paxton, and two or three other gents have gone down to New Mexico to hunt for the Last Chance gold. That's close to Elizabethtown, I think."

Jesse nodded, feeling his sagging spirits lift for the first time in months. "You're sure of this?"

"Fairly certain."

"Who gabbed?"

"Leo Moffat's wife."

"Moffat? The saloonkeeper over in Central City?"

"That's the one. His wife's helped me out more than once. So what d'you think? You going down there to look for 'em?"

Jesse took a long drag on his cigarette and thumped the ashes into a brass spittoon. "Damned right I am. This is the first solid lead I've had in months. I've got to get my hands on those two, collect my money, and move on to something else. I've been on Paxton's tail close to two years now."

"Him and Taylor've managed to stay one step ahead of the law for a long time. It's almost uncanny."

Jesse's hollow eyes took on a flinty cast in the dim light. "Their time's coming."

"Well, Jess, I wish you all the luck in your noble conquest. You're gonna need it," Bud said dryly and clinked his glass against Jesse's before draining it. "Vic Taylor's mean, and he's smart or he would've been bagged years ago."

"What's Paxton's excuse?"

"Now he's a hard one to figure. He's cut from a different mold. Too damned likable." Bud suddenly laughed. "Shell Paxton's the type who'll steal you blind, then turn right around and loan you enough of his own money to see you through till your next paycheck."

"He's got a conscience," Jesse admitted. "It's his weak point."

Bud shook his head. "No, Paxton's weak point is his sticky fingers. Chop off his hands, and you'd have an honest, law-abiding citizen."

"Think so?" Jesse grinned wolfishly. "Maybe when I catch up with him, I'll try that and see if it works."

Sally and a couple of friends spent the afternoon at the dressmaker's, chatting happily as they admired the latest fashions and felt samplings of material between their fingers. Hoop skirts and bustles were out; trim, figure-molding styles were in. Sally splurged and ordered a new hat and dress and hoped they would be ready by the time she saw Shell again.

To her friends, Sally Paxton, alias Sally Gibson, was a mystery. She lived alone in a small cottage on a quiet, tree-lined street in Denver, and while the ring on her finger proved she was married, her husband was a shadow in the dark. They never saw him. Sally sensed her friends' hungry curiosity but didn't feed it, willing to put up with their speculation and prying questions if it would protect Shell. She trusted no one.

Sally couldn't say with any honesty that she was happy, but she still tried to look on the bright side, telling herself that once she and Shell were together again everything would straighten out. They'd change their names, move someplace where no one knew them, and start a new life. But how long must she wait? Even if Shell and Vic found the Last Chance gold, they would have to sell it in Mexico. She might not see Shell for months to come, longer if Adam Chaney discovered they had found his gold and sicced the law after them. She almost hoped the bullion remained lost forever.

On the street where Sally Paxton lived, she enjoyed a breathtaking view of the snow-capped Rockies, and this evening they were particularly beautiful, with the sun just setting, melting it seemed, into their lofty summits. Tired from her afternoon outing, however, Sally hardly noticed them. She arrived home late, and she was alone, a combination she usually tried to avoid. Opening the door, she stepped into the cool darkness of her sitting room and was immediately confronted by the pleasant aroma of cooking food.

It shocked her. Someone was here! Sally's gaze went to the door leading to the kitchen. There was a light burning. Undecided whether she should investigate further or run, Sally fumbled in her purse with one hand for the derringer Shell had given her last Christmas, then remembered it was still lying on the table next to her bed and almost panicked.

Behind her, the sun made a final plunge into the mountains and was gone. So was Sally's courage. She backed silently toward the open doorway, out of the house, and whirled to leave.

"Hey, wait, Sally! It's just me!"

She stopped in her tracks, recognizing the voice, the faint English accent. Turning, she saw Leo Moffat.

Short and stocky, coarse, iron gray hair standing on end

like a porcupine's quills, he filled the doorway and wiped his hands dry. Sally noticed he was wearing one of her aprons, the pink one with all the ruffles, and laughed shakily as she neared the door again.

He smiled. "When you didn't come home, I got hungry and took over your kitchen. Hope you don't mind."

"Oh. No, not at all." Relieved, Sally pressed a hand to her forehead and let it slide down to her cheek as she followed him inside. "I couldn't imagine who was here."

Leo took her bonnet and shawl and seated her at the kitchen table. "How are you getting along?"

"I'm doing fine." She peeled off her kid gloves and smoothed them out against her thighs. "Considering you scared the blue blazes out of me."

Laughing more at her unladylike bluntness than anything, Leo set the table and pulled up a chair across from her. Sally watched him, puzzled, not sure why he was here and almost afraid to ask. He came to check on her every so often on Shell's behalf, but she sensed there was something more important behind this visit.

"Leo, what's wrong?"

"Nothing yet."

"Yet?"

"Let's eat first," he said. "Do you want gravy with that?"

"Leo, don't put me off. It's Shell, isn't it? Something's happened."

He sighed and laid down his fork. "Jesse Watts is here in Denver."

"What!"

Leo shrugged. "I wasn't really surprised when I found out. Vic and Shell are all over the newspapers, you know. Word has it, Watts has been in Colorado for some time now, trying to hunt them down."

"But here! In Denver! Do you think he knows about me?"

"Who's to say?"

Stunned, Sally rubbed her temples and gazed down at her plate of food.

"I don't think he'll bother you," Leo said after a moment. "I have a feeling he already knows Shell's in New Mexico."

She looked up at him. "How?"

"I'm almost ashamed to tell you," Leo said, and he appeared uncomfortable. "An ex-lawman by the name of Bud Thompson's been hanging around Central City a lot lately. He's a friend of Watts. The other day, I caught him at my house talking to my old lady and found out she's been feeding him information about Vic and Shell."

"Martha? But how would she know anything about them?"

"The rooms I rent out above the saloon—she comes in and cleans them when I'm too busy and washes the linens. I guess that's when she does her eavesdropping." Leo paused, pulling at his earlobe. "I knew she hated the company I kept but never thought she'd do a thing like this."

"You say this man is a friend of Jesse Watts?"

Leo nodded. "He'll tell Watts everything Martha said."

Sally was silent a moment, then suddenly leaning forward, she took one of Leo's hands in hers and squeezed it. "You have to help me."

"How?"

"We've got to get to Shell before Jesse Watts does."

"I'd like to, Sally, but I have my saloon to think of." He shook his head. "I can't leave it."

"Then I'll go myself."

Leo scowled. "You'll do no such thing."

"Oh? And who's gonna stop me?"

"I will, even if I have to hog-tie you to do it."

114

"You wouldn't dare."

Irritated, he laid down his knife and fork and fixed her with a steady gaze. "Stop being so bloody obstinate, will you? There's nothing you can do."

"Tell me how to get to the Last Chance Mine and Devil's Canyon."

"Shut up and eat before your food gets cold."

"I'm going, Leo. With or without your help."

"You'd never make it."

Sally's eyebrows lifted. "Why? Because I'm a woman? You'll have to come up with a better excuse than that," she said staunchly. "I'm not a city girl anymore, Leo, and I'm not weak. The hard work me and Shell did before we lost our land makes this jaunt to New Mexico sound like a Sunday picnic."

Surprised by her outburst, Leo didn't say anything for a long moment. When he did, his usual gruff tone of voice had softened. "You lost a baby boy because of all that hard work, too," he said, "and it's a wonder your little girl . . ." He paused. "I'm sorry, Sally. I forgot."

She shook her head. "It's all right. It's the truth. But I'm not expecting now, and I've got to find Shell and warn him." She forced a smile she did not feel. "I may not be another Daniel Boone, but I'd certainly survive longer than a certain saloonkeeper I know. Would you believe he never sets foot out of doors except for a random trip to the privy?"

Leo laughed. "You know, the more I listen to you, the more I begin to think my old lady's not such a battle-ax, after all."

"So will you help me?"

"I guess so, seeing as how your mind's made up. I'll go with you as far as E'town, and I'll ask around and find out the easiest route to Devil's Canyon, but after that, you're on your own." He paused, studying her. "Understand now, I'd go

115

myself if I could get away for any length of time."

Sally nodded, though she doubted it. Leo Moffat hated to ride horseback and rarely went anywhere if he couldn't go by rail or by stagecoach at the very least.

"You'll have to have fare for the train ride to New Mexico," he said, "and you'll need supplies once you get there. How are you fixed for money?"

"I've saved most of what Shell's sent me since he joined up with Vic."

"Good for you. Vic gives him a pretty decent cut, doesn't he?"

Sally made a face. "If Shell kisses his butt enough, he does."

"Ah, Sally . . ."

"Don't ah, Sally me," she snapped. "You know it's true."

Leo shook his finger at her. "I also know Shell's a good one for slipping gold watches and diamond rings into his pockets when Vic's not looking. He gets his fair share of the loot . . . one way or another."

Sally shrugged and picked at her food, not wanting to talk about it anymore. If holding out on Vic was the only way Shell could get his "fair share," then so be it. No doubt, he had learned how it was done from the very best.

Suddenly aware that she could hardly see to eat, Sally swiped at her eyes, angry that she was crying. It wasn't like her. Everything was so wrong, and while she had put up a brave front for Leo Moffat's benefit, she wasn't at all sure if she could do this.

She felt helpless. And alone.

CHAPTER THIRTEEN

The rain started out as a slow, cold drizzle during the night, strengthened to a regular downpour, then turned to driving sleet before daylight. Even with warm clothing and slickers, the men were soaked to the skin and half-frozen by the time they saddled up and headed out, and the heavy clouds overhead showed no signs of clearing.

The four treasure seekers pointed their horses south, following the same route another unfortunate party of men had chosen years ago. Shell thought of the similarities between themselves and Malo Chavez's men. Both were—or had been—cold, miserable, trailed by Adam Chaney, and driven by gold. A band of thieves following in the footsteps of a band of thieves.

Shell shook the ice from his bandana and tied it over his nose and mouth to block out some of the cold. He wasn't sure if it was May or June, but either way it was too late in spring to have icicles hanging off his nose.

He caught up with Vic. "Maybe we oughta find a place to hole up till this clears out."

Vic shook his head and glanced over at him. "You'll live," he said gruffly. Sleet clung to his brushy eyebrows and mustache, giving his face a frosty appearance. "We'll make Devil's Canyon by noon. We'll rest then."

Shell dropped back again and hunched his shoulders against the cold. Snip's shod hooves rang solidly on the frozen ground. Next to him, Darby was leading their mules and cursing the weather in short, angry bursts each time one of the mules balked or slipped on the ice.

117

Shell could feel the wind gradually picking up, pushing at his back and whipping Snip's tail around her hindlegs, and was reminded of the time a blizzard caught him a couple of miles from home when they lived in Texas. There'd been nothing to do but keep riding in what he had hoped was the right direction until he either stumbled into something or dropped dead. What he did was get tangled up in Sally's clothesline.

That one bad blizzard had marked the beginning of the end of his short career as a rancher. After the storm, he had found a number of his cows dead and had put several more out of their miseries when he discovered their feet had frozen. The memory of it left a pained expression on his face.

Darby noticed it. "You all right?"

He nodded and tugged his bandana higher.

By mid morning, it had stopped sleeting, allowing them a clearer view of the country around them. Needing fresh meat, the men kept an eye out for game, and Vic casually pointed to four or five elk outlined on a ridge about a half mile away. They were out of range, but trigger-happy Joe hiked up his rifle and took aim and shot before anyone could stop him. The elk bounded into the trees unharmed as the blast echoed like cannon fire across the meadow.

Eyes blazing, Vic wrenched the rifle from Joe's hands. "Finney, if you were any damned dumber, you'd be dangerous!" He emptied the cartridges from the magazine tube, dropped them into his coat pocket, and tossed the rifle back to Joe. "Don't fire it again until I say to!"

Joe bristled. "Listen here, grandpa . . ."

Vic turned on him, and Joe apparently forgot what he was about to say. He shoved his rifle back into the boot.

"Anymore lip out of you today, and I'll kill you," Vic promised. "Got that?"

Hat brim flapping in the wind, Joe glared at him but had sense enough not to mouth off. He and Darby both had come to take Vic at his word.

Feeling as if his butt was frozen to the saddle, Shell finally spoke up. "It's not gettin' any warmer. Shouldn't we be moving on?"

Vic nodded and led the way.

Slowed by the weather, they didn't reach Devil's Canyon until much later that afternoon, and it was some of the rawest country Shell had seen in days. Stopping his horse beneath a wind-blasted conifer at the canyon's rim, he looked down and gasped. It was a sheer drop, straight down, with nothing but the skeleton-like arms of dead, barkless trees to catch you before you hit the boulders far below. The whole canyon floor—as much of it as he could see at least—was strewn with uprooted aspen and pine and great slabs of rock that had broken off the surrounding cliffs. Over it all, the ice gleamed and crackled, beautiful to see, but as sharp to the touch as slivers of broken glass.

Darby drew up beside him and frowned, not happy with what he saw. "There's no way down!" He had to shout above the howling wind. "Betcha we'll have to ride another ten, fifteen miles just to find an opening!"

Vic stood up in his stirrups, searching for the landmarks Malo Chavez had told him were there. On their left flank, the land fell away sharply, but whatever lay below was hidden by dense timber. Vic, however, seemed to recognize it. He shouted and motioned for them to follow him.

Halfway down the slope, they struck an old trail that wound through the trees, deeper and deeper, until the wind could no longer touch them. When the trail widened into the mouth of a rocky gulch, the men dismounted and continued downward, more cautiously now, not sure where its twisting course would end. Surprisingly, the gulch led them straight through the wall of the canyon itself, a slit-like pass barely wide enough for them to walk through single file. Rock walls towered hundreds of feet above their heads and closed in on them so that it was like walking through a tunnel, and Shell tried not to think what would become of them if a flash flood suddenly crashed in on them from behind. Frightened by the limited space and darkness, the horses shied and rolled their eyes. The pass descended so sharply at times that they were forced to sit on their haunches to keep from tumbling.

The defile began to widen little by little, and Shell was grateful to see daylight shining on the walls ahead of him. When at last he led Snip out into the open, he found himself on the canyon floor among the same deadfall and tumbled boulders he had seen from above.

Joe and Darby spotted a crude cross not far from the canyon's mouth, marking a grave. The body had evidently been tucked beneath a low ledge where it was then covered over with rocks and clay. It was just the first of many old graves they would find in Devil's Canyon.

Mounting up, Vic looked over at Shell. "There's supposed to be a spring and a little shelter on down the canyon a ways. Might make it before dark if we hurry."

Shell merely nodded, not trusting his voice. He was shivering uncontrollably in his damp clothes.

He fell in behind Vic, and without knowing why or thinking about it, looked straight up at the place on the cliff where he had stood only minutes ago. He pulled up so short his mount slipped and almost fell.

A man on horseback was outlined clearly against the pale sky, black, silent, motionless, but before Shell could react or say a word, he was gone. In the blink of an eye, both man and horse had faded into the background and disappeared.

Or had they been there at all? Shell squinted up at the empty cliff and didn't know. He was beginning to doubt his own senses.

"Water's boiling! Quit lovin' up on that broomtail and make us some coffee!"

Vic's voice grated on Shell's nerves. Disregarding the order, he pulled up more grass, beat the ice out of it, and added it to the pile he had already gathered, making sure Snip had enough feed to last her for at least a few hours. The ice cut the horses' and mules' mouths when they tried to graze on their own.

Enjoying the solitude, if not the cold, he dawdled a moment longer and fed the mare another handful of grain, listening to the hollow crunch of her teeth. The night was so black, he could see little more of her than the patch of white on her muzzle as she shoved it into his cupped palm.

"Hey, Shell! What the devil are you doing?"

Swearing under his breath, Shell left the horses, ducked beneath the rock overhang that sheltered their camp, and pitched his gloves next to his gear. The smell of burning pine perfumed the air, and there were smoke smudges on the rock above them, indicating they weren't the first party to have camped here within the last few years.

Shell knelt beside the fire and dumped a measure of coffee into the pot of hot water. "That was sure as hell hard," he said irritably. "I'll have to give lessons someday."

Vic ignored Shell's unusual show of anger. "You make coffee like my ma used to," he said. "Not too strong, not too weak." Standing stooped beneath the lower end of the overhang with the three skinny rabbits Joe had shot earlier dangling from his left hand, he looked down on Shell and frowned. "Get out of them damp clothes and warm up 'fore

you catch your death. Me and the boy'll skin out these rabbits."

Shell stripped down, still shivering, feeling the chill
working its way into his bones. Wrapped in a wool blanket, he
spread his jeans, shirt, and underwear on the rocks nearest
the fire to dry and put on a fresh change of clothes.

Joe looked over at him, his eyes alight with deviltry. "Cold
night like this, I bet you miss your woman, eh, Tex?" He was
sprawled next to the fire in his long johns with both feet extended dangerously close to the flames, skinny toes spread
wide and wriggling like worms. "She sure is a cute little
thing," he went on. "Reminds me of a gal used to work in
Leadville a few years back. If I remember right, her name was
Sally, too." Joe suddenly grinned. "She was just a slip of a girl
but almighty soft and warm, I'll tell you."

Shell felt his insides tighten. Eyes lowered, jaws knotted,
he finished buttoning his shirt and tucked the tail into his
pants, aware all the while of Joe's amused stare. He had an
overwhelming urge to kick the man's head in, an impulse that
shocked him the second he thought it. Squatting by the fire,
he gave the red coals a few vigorous jabs with a stick, wishing
a spark would fly up and burn a nice big hole in the bottom of
one of Joe Finney's feet.

Joe sat up and peered over the flames at him. "You and
your wife have any kids?"

"We did," he murmured.

"Really? Do you ever get a little suspicious?"

Shell eyed him from beneath lowered brows, waiting for
the punch line.

"I mean, given your wife's background and all," Joe
sneered, "how do you know the brats are even yours?"

Except for a subtle paling of the skin around his mouth,
Shell's face remained unchanged. Yet something inside him

snapped. Wiping his hands on his pants, he slowly rose, looked down on Joe's smug face, and very calmly raked his foot through the fire and kicked a bucket's worth of coals and burning wood into the man's lap.

Whatever Joe had expected him to do, it wasn't this. Yelling and frantically brushing and beating at his smoking underwear, he scrambled away from the scattered embers, and Darby ran forward and doused him with water. Shell wasn't far behind him.

Stepping around the fire, he shouldered past Darby, grasped Joe Finney by the hair with one hand, and punched him in the mouth with the other, then shoved him against the back wall of the overhang.

It took Joe a moment to realize what had happened. Touching a hand to his broken lips, he glanced down at the blood on his fingers and went berserk. His eyes glazed over with hatred.

Shell was closing in on him but never saw it coming. Bounding away from the wall, Joe hurtled forward like a run-away locomotive and lit into him with gritted teeth and lightning fists, his first blow catching him on the jaw. Every tooth in Shell's head rattled. He staggered back a step, one whole side of his face feeling as if it had been swiped clean off, and Joe followed him up and struck again, his knuckles plowing across Shell's cheekbone and breaking the skin.

Still recovering from the first blow, Shell barely ducked the third, shifted his weight to the side, and kicked Joe in the kneecap. He heard a distinctive pop and a groan as Joe grabbed at his knee, and made good use of an unexpected opportunity.

Moving in close, he gripped Joe by the throat, hard, flexed fingers digging in deeply, squeezing the man's gullet as he drove him backwards and slammed him against the rock wall.

He punched Joe over and over in the gut, nostrils flaring, lips drawn back from his teeth, and his every move was clean and swift and packed with a hidden strength that surprised them both.

Joe's face turned red, then a deep purple as he struggled to breathe, and still Shell held on to him, cutting off his wind with one hand while he pounded away at him with his left fist and watched an expression of panic creep into the man's eyes. He felt Darby trying to force them apart, felt Joe clawing at the hand at his throat and heard him gasping for air, but was strangely distanced from it all. It was as if he played no part in it, an innocent bystander to his own ferocity.

Under Darby James' persistent prying, however, Shell's bulldog hold on Joe's throat began to slip, and he gave the man one more bruise to remember him by before releasing him. Hoisting Finney's limp body up by the front of his long johns, he rammed a knee into his crotch, took better aim, and kneed him again, dead center.

A raspy bawl burst from Joe's tortured throat as he slid to the ground. Coughing and gagging, he cupped both hands over his groin while the pain knifed upwards and twisted his face into a tight grimace.

Keeping an eye on Darby, Shell circled Joe Finney, wary and waiting, and blew his breath on the raw knuckles of his left hand. When he was certain he had beaten the fight out of Joe, his anger ebbed to a slow burn.

"You girls kiss and make up now," Vic said cheerfully. He was lounging by the fire on his blankets and had watched the entire scuffle in quiet amusement. He motioned to Shell. "Come on, kid. He's had enough."

Backing off, Shell turned and found himself face to face with Darby James. He spat blood, wiped his mouth. "Are you next?"

"Huh?" The boy looked startled. "I got no quarrel with you."

"Then get the hell out of my way."

CHAPTER FOURTEEN

The day had been long and hard, and no one felt like standing guard that night. Bringing the animals in off the grass, Vic and Darby picketed them close to camp, wrapped up in their blankets, and died the instant their heads touched the ground.

Exhausted as they were, Joe and Shell had a more difficult time falling asleep, each man too distrustful of the other to close his eyes. Tired of it, Shell finally drew his Colt from the holster and snuggled it next to him under the blankets. Watching him, Joe did likewise and was soon snoring.

Shell kept an eye on him a long while, making sure he was really asleep, and rested a hand on his gun. He couldn't relax. His thoughts kept returning to Joe's caustic remark about Sally. Shell didn't always understand his wife, but he knew her well enough to be certain that whatever else she may have done in Leadville, she had never been a prostitute. Yet the cut continued to fester.

It wasn't like Shell to brood over something of such little consequence. He sensed the difference. The protective wall he had built up around himself so many years ago was crumbling apart bit by bit. He could feel it breaking away, eroding under the barrage of insults, gibes, and jabs that had been hurled his way unchecked for much too long. He was beginning to feel their sting.

Shell drifted off to sleep at last, only to be jolted back out of it a few hours later by a deep, racking cough that sent him after his whiskey. He whipped off the covers and fumbled the bottle from his saddlebag.

His mouth full of liquor, Shell looked around him in surprise. It was snowing. Light flurries of it whirled beneath the overhang at regular intervals and hissed softly on the few remaining coals of their fire. The cold, clean whiteness of it lit up the night.

Shell's cough gradually slacked off, and he shook the snow from his covers and combed it out of his hair with his fingers. Not far from him, Vic was sleeping soundly, his breathing slow and deep, and Shell noticed then that Joe's bed was empty.

Setting the bottle aside, he reached for his gun and started to rise.

"Does this weather beat anything you ever saw or what?" Darby James was sitting up within the deeper shadows of the overhang, watching him intently. "Seems like winter ain't ready to call it quits."

"Where's Joe?" Shell whispered.

Darby hesitated, then shrugged. "Better get some wood on that fire," he said and got to his feet.

"Where is he, Darby?"

The boy raked the coals together, added kindling, and waited for it to flare up. "Joe's answering nature's call, most likely." He looked over at Shell and grinned. "He'd better hurry. Liable to freeze something off."

Shell made no comment. Sitting cross-legged, he threw a blanket over his head, snugged it tightly under his chin, and stared out into the night. He could see the horses standing with their heads down and tails tucked while the silent snow coated their backs and clung to them in frozen clumps. This was, he knew, Old Man Winter's last gasp and would soon pass away, but even so, he found himself thinking more and more of his and Sally's dashed plans to resettle in sunny Arizona. He was having a hard time lately remembering the

127

purpose for his being here in the first place.

"You might as well go back to sleep," Darby whispered. "Joe said he wanted to check on the horses and mules and take a look around. He won't be back for a little while."

On the rock above Shell's head, a number of long icicles gleamed in the firelight, and he counted them one last time before tearing his eyes away to look at the boy.

"I'll wait."

"What's wrong? You think he'd shoot you while you're asleep?"

"Wouldn't surprise me none."

Darby dropped down beside him and tucked his knees up under his chin. "Man, you really kicked his ass," he said. "I thought you were gonna kill him."

"So did I."

They fell silent, passing the whiskey bottle back and forth, each busy with his own thoughts. Joe Finney's absence made Shell uneasy. Ever since that day Joe had shot at him, he had made it a point to know where he was and what he was doing at all times. The longer he stayed gone, the more Shell suspected he was up to no good. But what that might be, he couldn't guess.

Warmed by the fire, an icicle broke loose from the overhang and shattered like glass against the frozen ground. Hearing it, Vic stirred and mumbled something in his sleep.

Shell glanced up. "Only sixteen more to go," he said idly.

"Sixteen what?"

"Icicles."

Darby studied him, frowned, and looked back into the bright flames of their fire. "When do you think we'll find the gold?"

"No telling. Maybe never."

"Do you know where it is?"

"No."

Darby nodded. "That's what I told Joe. You know what's gonna happen, don't you? Vic'll try to take his share and ours, too."

A smile touched the corners of Shell's mouth. "But you and Finney would never sink that low, right?"

"Go ahead and scoff," Darby said. "Maybe you don't know it, but you're the one that'll get caught in the middle."

"How do you figure that?"

"I just know." He spat into the fire and listened to it sizzle, then glanced over at Shell. "You saw him, didn't you?"

"Who?"

"Adam Chaney."

Shell met his gaze. "Right after we rode into the canyon, I saw somebody on the cliff above us. Or thought I did."

"It was him all right. Listen, Shell, I'm not supposed to be telling you this, but me and Joe . . . we've got an ace in the hole you don't know about."

"Adam Chaney have something to do with it?"

"Maybe. Maybe not."

Shell coughed, muffling the sound with his hand so as not to awaken Vic, swallowed another long, hot swig of whiskey, and passed the bottle to Darby. "So in other words," he said, "you wouldn't tell me the truth even if he did."

"Look, all I'm trying to do is warn you before it's too late. Get out now while the gettin's good." Darby paused to drink and gave him a sidelong look. "Joe's dead set on keeping the gold from you and Vic. And he'll do it, too."

"Why are you telling me this, Darby? You think I'm so dumb I don't know what's at stake?"

"No, it's just that there's more to this than meets the eye. The chips are stacked against you." He nodded at Vic Taylor. "I don't give a tinker's damn what happens to him. Only reason I've put up with his bullshit all these months is because of the gold. He knows where it's hid. We don't. Soon as he finds it . . . ." Darby pretended his hand was a gun and aimed at Vic. "Bang. He's out of the picture, and Joe'll see to it that you are, too, if you stick around." He paused, resting his chin on upraised knees. "This ain't my idea, you understand. I mean, it's like I told you before. I got nothing against you."

"Like hell."

Frowning, Darby looked over at him. "Why else would I tell you all this?"

"To scare me off." Shell drained the last of the whiskey and pitched the empty bottle into a nearby bush. "In case you didn't know it," he said, "I didn't make this trip for the fun of it. I'm here for the gold, and I'll fight for my share."

"Would you fight Vic Taylor for it?"

Shell's gaze touched Vic, then settled back on the boy, a tell-nothing expression on his face, in his eyes. "I said I'd fight."

Darby shook his head. "But you won't go against Vic. You're afraid of him." He got to his feet and stretched. "Take my advice, Shell, and get out. You can't win."

"And what makes you think you will?"

"It's in the bag," he said simply and started to leave. "I'm gonna go see what's keeping Joe."

"Darby." Shell waited for the boy to turn and look back at him. "If you know something, something about Adam Chaney, anything, you'd better spit it out."

The boy grinned. "Chaney? Never heard of him," he declared and sauntered away, his footsteps sounding gritty in the fresh-fallen snow.

It was clearly a taunt. Shell watched him until he disappeared into the darkness and wondered. What was Darby

James hiding? Did Chaney have anything to do with it? Shell doubted it and had a feeling the whole conversation had been set up to scare him into leaving. After all, the less people there were, the more gold each man would get. And Vic would be outnumbered two to one if it came down to a fight.

But what if he was wrong and there was, in fact, more to it than that, as Darby had suggested?

Half-drunk and too tired to think, Shell rested his forehead against his open palm and closed his eyes. He gingerly felt of the bruise and scabbed-over gash on his cheekbone where Joe Finney's knuckles had broken the skin. It was painful to the touch.

"You and the boy seem to be getting along better these days."

At the sound of Vic's voice, Shell jerked his head up. It took his eyes a moment to focus. "What?"

Vic sat up and tugged on his boots. "I thought you knew I was a light sleeper," he said.

"So you heard."

"I heard most of it."

Shell hesitated, uncertain, then asked, "What do you think?"

Vic shrugged indifferently. "I told you a long time ago it'd be dog-eat-dog once we found the gold."

"I'm talking about Adam Chaney."

"He's the least of our problems." Vic rubbed his big hands together briskly and warmed them over the fire. "Darb threw Chaney in to worry you, and you fell for it hook, line, and sinker. You're too damned gullible."

"I don't like surprises."

Vic glanced up at Shell, caught the suspicious look in his eyes, and scowled. "What the hell's the matter with you? You really think I want your share?"

"You tell me," Shell said, his voice quiet, steady.

The two men stared at each other a long moment, one a leader, the second a follower who only lately had begun to question the other's lifelong control over him. Vic's grip was slipping, but Shell still couldn't quite break free. The habit was too strong.

Feeling his face heat up, he looked away first and gazed down at his hands. Vic's black eyes glinted in the firelight like small, wet stones.

"You know better than to cross me, Shell," he said at length. "But I'll give you the benefit of the doubt this time and assume it's the liquor talking and not you." Hearing Joe Finney and Darby James approaching, Vic rose and looked down on Shell's bowed head. "You'd better figure out who's side you're on, kid. Straddling fences ain't healthy."

CHAPTER FIFTEEN

"If Shell knew I was letting you do this, he'd have my hair."

They were standing in front of the Humbug Livery Stable at the edge of Elizabethtown in the cold calm of early morning. The peaks of McGinty and Baldy mountains were huddled around them like sleeping giants.

Decked out in her husband's cast-off clothes and a wide-brimmed hat, Sally Paxton finished adjusting the saddle stirrups and looked over her mount's back at Leo. "Shell knows I can take care of myself," she said.

"This is different than some dance hall up to Leadville," Leo argued. Squinting at her through myopic eyes, he bit the end off a fresh cigar and spit it out with more force than was necessary. "You ought to be at home polishing the silverware or something."

"And let Shell be killed by a bloodthirsty bounty hunter without even trying to help him?" She shook her head. "I won't sit back and let it happen."

Leo scowled. "The train leaves in an hour, Sally. Forget this foolishness and ride back with me to Central City."

"And do what?"

"Wait. Wait and hope everything turns out all right."

Sally sighed. She was tired of waiting. Hadn't she done just that all winter? It had been months since she had seen her husband, and if Jesse Watts found him, she might never see him again. She knew this was the only course left for her to follow.

"Leo, you're wasting your breath," she said at last. "If I lose Shell, I lose everything."

She left him to watch the horses and walked back into the livery stable for the rest of her gear, glancing up at the huge, black and white sign above the door as she entered. It read: We Buy, Sell, Trade, and Rent. Your Satisfaction is Guaranteed.

Sally hoped so.

The two horses she had rented appeared to be in good shape, but neither she nor Leo knew what conformities to look for in them. If Shell was here he would know, she thought, and wished she had paid more attention the times he had bought horses back home. She was almost certain the pack horse had what Shell would call bandy legs, but whether that would have any effect on the animal's usefulness or not she couldn't guess.

It was touch-and-go from here on. She would have to take her chances.

Slinging the saddlebags over her shoulder, Sally looked at the list of supplies she had written out during the train ride from Denver. With Leo's help, she had narrowed it down to the bare necessities so that the load was much lighter than it would have been otherwise. Leo had ignored her objections and had bought her a good rifle. She picked it up now, liking the feel of it and the handsome walnut stock. It was a Colt Lightning Slide-Action, .44-40 caliber, and weighed less than six pounds, making it easier for her to handle.

"Going on a hunting trip?"

Startled, Sally turned and saw it was the stablehand.

"I guess you could say that," she replied.

"Fishing's what I like," he told her. "These mountain streams are cram-full of trout."

Not knowing what else to say, Sally merely smiled.

He watched her gather her supplies and leaned against the door frame. "Ma'am, I don't mean to stick my nose where it don't belong, but I overheard you say something to the gentleman outside about Devil's Canyon. That where you're headed?"

"I haven't decided," she said cautiously.

He shook his head and frowned. "That's some mighty rough country. I hate the thought of any woman riding out that way by herself. It ain't safe." He leaned to the side to spit and scuffed dirt and loose fodder over it. "Fact is," he added, "it ain't safe for nobody, man or woman either one."

Sally's brows lifted. "Because of Adam Chaney, you mean?"

"Well, yeah, there's old Adam, but he's not the only one you have to look out for. We've had some rough-looking characters pass through here lately."

"Oh?"

He nodded. "A few days ago, four men stopped by here and bought some grain for their horses." He gave her a knowing look. "I'd bet my wife and kids they were on the dodge. They didn't ride through town. Stayed plumb clear of it, like they didn't want anyone to see 'em. Being curious, I watched them leave and noticed they took the old road to Last Chance. That's the one you'll likely take if you're going to Devil's Canyon."

Suddenly interested, Sally took a step toward him. "You said there were four men. Can you remember what they looked like?"

"It was pretty early when they stopped by . . . and dark." He squinted one eye, thinking, shaking his head. His stooped shoulders lifted and fell. "Can't remember nary a thing about them, except the one that bought the grain. A tough-talking, blond-haired kid. Kind of stocky built and mean in the eyes. You know the type."

She nodded, sure he had described Darby James. "You

don't remember anything else?"

"No, ma'am, but it's like I told you. These fellas weren't Sunday school teachers."

Sally had to smile, thinking of Shell with his good looks and nice, quiet manners. The suspicious stablehand probably would have thought them outlaws even if they had been a party of circuit-riding preachers.

"Then there was this other stranger," the stablehand was saying, "come through here asking questions about that bunch I just told you about." He paused to bite off a good-sized chaw of tobacco. Eyes wide, heart thumping, Sally waited impatiently for him to finish maneuvering it around inside his cheek so he could talk. "Had his horse shipped down here from Denver I believe it was," he continued. "Fine-looking critter, I'll tell you."

"But the man . . ."

"He lit out after the first four."

"A tall man with a black beard?"

The stablehand looked at her, surprised. "Why, yes, ma'am. How'd you know that?"

"What day did he leave?"

"Oh, he took off yesterday afternoon." He studied her curiously. "Why? Do you know him?"

"Yes, I do," she said. "You've been a big help. Thank you."

Before he could ask any more questions, she pushed past him and hurried outside. The bounty hunter had been here. Had already come and gone.

Sally feared that she was not going to reach Shell in time to save him from Jesse Watts . . . and even more importantly, from Vic Taylor. In truth, she distrusted Vic more than the manhunter. At least Jesse Watts' motives were clear. Vic, on the other hand, was sneaky, deceitful. Yet Sally had never been fooled by his slick talk, had never liked him, and blamed him for much of their present dilemma. If not for this one man, she felt sure that Shell would not have turned into an outlaw.

How Shell could continue to revere Vic as his friend, advisor, and father-figure after all the trouble he had caused them, Sally didn't know. Her husband's ordinarily good judge of character and rationality tended to cloud wherever Vic was concerned.

All the more reason for her to be there to protect him from the big man's influence and violent temper. Their future together depended upon her now. Clearly, she hadn't a minute to lose.

The taste of the hunt was hot on Jesse's tongue.

Without realizing it, Shell Paxton had done exactly what he swore he would never do and had led him straight to Old Man Taylor himself, and Jesse was gaining ground hour by hour, day by day. Closing in for the kill.

He had taken the time to carefully study the four outlaws' trail and had come to recognize and distinguish not only the tracks of the horses they rode, but the footprints of the men, as well. He had matched up each print with the person he thought had made it, from Taylor's huge, run-over boots to Joe Finney's splay-footed walk, and by studying the sign left behind at the men's campsites, he began to slowly pick up on their individual routines and habits. It helped him to better know and understand the men themselves.

Perhaps because of his particular grudge against the man, Shell Paxton interested him most. For whatever reason, Paxton seemed to keep to himself both on the trail and in camp and, unless Jesse was mistaken, served as the eyes and ears for the entire party. On the bank of the Rio Colorado, he found where Paxton had cut off from the main trail and had reined his mount into the denser trees and undergrowth, obviously seeking cover from something or someone on the opposite bank. Out of curiosity, Jesse crossed the rushing stream, tethered his horse, and scouted around on foot until, halfway up the mountain slope, he found what had alerted Paxton.

A new set of footprints, ill-defined but deep in the loose earth, proved there had been someone up there. Jesse found where the man had crouched down among the pines to watch the riders below him. He combed the area for empty cartridge shells, anything to suggest there might have been shots exchanged, but found nothing. It was evident, however, that the two men were far from friendly.

So who was the man on the slope? And why was he trailing Taylor's gang? For the gold, or for the bounty? Or both?

Pondering this, Jesse remembered Adam Chaney and had almost concluded it must be him, when he made another puzzling discovery.

The weather turned wet and cold, and Jesse lost the outlaws' trail. Cursing his luck, he continued southward, hoping to find the narrow, slit-like entrance to Devil's Canyon that one of the old-timers back in Elizabethtown had told him about. Unfortunately, the terrain looked much different covered in a blanket of snow, and it wasn't until late the next day that he finally located the cleft.

He stumbled onto a single set of hoofprints in the canyon the following morning. Though the snow was starting to melt in the bottoms, the trail was plain, and he followed it for a quarter of a mile to where the rider had dismounted and met with another man on foot. Swinging out of the saddle, Jesse studied the new set of tracks, noting the way the toes turned outwards. Joe Finney.

It appeared the strange horseman and Finney had talked for quite some time, judging by the number of cigarette butts, then both men had parted ways, the horseman riding due east toward a narrow side canyon, while Finney walked back the way he had come. Following the trail, Jesse found where someone had joined Finney and walked with him to the now abandoned camp beneath the overhang, smaller footprints this time, either the James boy or Shell Paxton; the tracks were too old and poorly defined for Jesse to be sure.

More questions surfaced. Was this horseman the same man whom Paxton had seen earlier on the Rio Colorado? If so, what link did he have with Joe Finney? Going over the different sets of tracks again, he noticed that, twice, Finney had stumbled into small clumps of brush, leading him to believe that the meeting between Finney and the horseman had been at night. Had it also been in secret?

Jesse believed so.

Mounting up, he looked around him at the wild, raw land, eyes narrowed to slits against the glare of sunlight on snow. He had seen situations like this before. Gold had a way of tearing partnerships all to hell, and if he was reading the signs right, this one was already cracked down the middle.

It was Jesse's belief that the man who played a lone hand usually came out on top. Confident, he smiled and touched a spur to the dun gelding's side.

The bounty and the gold. His payday was becoming even more lucrative than he had imagined.

CHAPTER SIXTEEN

Devil's Canyon wasn't a single canyon, but a maze of canyons and gorges, twisting, winding, branching off, sometimes narrow, sometimes wide, but always deep and formidable.

With the snow melting and the spring rains pouring, the four outlaws' progress was slowed by mud and interrupted more than once by fallen timber. Slides had uprooted many of the pines and aspens on the steep slopes and had dumped them into the bottoms, often blocking their route, and the deadfall had to be dragged out of the way with the mules. It was hard, time-consuming work, and Shell Paxton figured if they ever found the Last Chance gold, they would have earned every ounce of it.

It was during one of these snags that he began to wonder if Vic even knew where they were.

They had hit a particularly bad pileup of logs and had worked half the morning clearing a path. Caked in mud and sweat, Shell began reloading the packs on the mules and was fumbling with stiff fingers at the knots and buckles when Darby came striding up to him, his face red with anger.

"That old codger went and led us down the wrong trail!" he exclaimed and waved an arm at the timber they had just finished dragging aside. "We moved that mess all for nothing! Gotta turn right around and backtrack five miles or more."

Shell received the news without comment. He didn't even bother to look up from his work.

While he, Darby, and Joe were busy clearing deadfall, Vic had walked down canyon a way, searching for familiar landmarks. He must not have found any. Shell could hear him arguing with Joe Finney now.

Joe was still suffering from the fight under the overhang. His voice sounded raspy and weak, and he rarely talked now unless his dander was up, which was enough. His knee was troubling him, too, and was so swollen the day after the fight that he had been forced to cut his pants open to relieve the pressure. Shell, however, felt neither guilt nor concern for his misery.

Fuming, Darby helped him with the packs. "Vic never should've burned that map," he said. "Now we probably won't find the gold. Or if we do, we'll all be so derned old we won't get to have any fun with it." He paused in his tirade to look at Shell. "Well, ain't you got anything to say?"

"No." Shell had stopped taking things for granted a long time ago.

The boy swore. "Might as well be talking to a fence post," he grumbled, but continued anyway. "I'll tell you what I think. I think he's gone and got us lost."

Shell still didn't respond, keeping his thoughts to himself as usual. They could talk about this all day, but it wouldn't get them any closer to the gold, nor would it bring back the time they had lost in clearing the wrong trail.

Once the mules were ready, he slopped through the mud to his horse and swung into the saddle. Vic had already led off and was some distance ahead of them, retracing the trail they had made earlier that morning.

Except for an occasional afternoon shower, the weather had turned off fair and warm since the snowstorm, but the canyon was so deep in places that the sun never touched the bottom until high noon, creating discomforts of two extremes. The men froze in the mornings and fried in the afternoons. And then, of course, there were the flies. About the time the temperature reached a comfortable degree, biting black flies appeared in swarms and gave neither man nor beast a minute of peace.

Shell slapped at his neck, killing just one of many that had sank its teeth into him in the last half hour, and spoke to the mare. Snip disliked the muddy footing and let him know it every step of the way, fighting the bit and sometimes crow-hopping as if she might like to throw him in the middle of it.

He finally urged her into a plodding canter and caught up with Vic. They rode side by side without speaking.

Shell looked around him. They were starting to leave the high country behind them. Blue spruce and aspen had thinned out and disappeared, and ponderosa pine was very slowly giving way to more and more piñon.

Vic shaded his face and squinted up at the towering red cliffs. "That gold's so close, I can smell it," he murmured.

The big man seemed to be talking more to himself than anyone, so Shell kept quiet. He followed his gaze to a huge lichen-covered boulder ahead of them. The boulder was split down the middle and a scraggly oak had taken root in the crack where water and soil had collected. It was a strange sight, and when they reached it, Vic drew rein. Shell remembered they had stopped here earlier this morning.

Dismounting, Vic stumbled over the talus around the split boulder until he was standing in the meager shade of the oak. He scanned the rocky wall on the opposite side of the canyon. "Damn thing has to be here somewhere," he said, sounding as if he were still talking to himself.

"What are you looking for?"

Vic glanced his way. By the expression on his face, Shell thought that he had only now noticed his presence.

"What do you think I'm looking for?" he asked. "I'm looking for the cave Malo and his boys were holed up in." Still gazing at the canyon wall, he fumbled in his shirt pocket and drew out a piece of candy. "Malo told me to keep an eye out for a big, split rock. From this point, he claimed if I looked down the canyon I'd be able to see the cave's mouth. It's about midway up the wall and angles inward so you can't see it unless you're standing off to the side. He said it was easier to spot from a distance than up close."

Shell looked but saw nothing except slabs of bare rocks and stunted pines. It seemed to him an unlikely place to find a cave, considering they had passed up a dozen or more clearly visible ones in the last three days.

It had been twenty some-odd years since Malo Chavez stashed his gold and fled these rugged mountains and canyon lands for the safety of Mexico. Twenty years. That was a long gap, and Shell wondered if the lapse of time might have affected Chavez's memory. If not his memory, then what about the land itself? It probably looked different now than it had when Chavez passed through. Small trees were large now. Older trees were dead. Landslides, flash floods, and fires could destroy in seconds what had taken years to form.

Vic seemed to read his thoughts. "Except for this split rock, the landmarks Malo told me to look for are gone. That's why I passed it up this morning." He paused, chewing his candy and sucking his teeth, thinking. "Might as well take a closer look," he said finally and glanced at Shell. "What do you think?"

"Suits me," he answered, surprised Vic would bother to ask him what he thought of anything.

Joe Finney had ridden up and was listening intently. He scowled. "This better not be another wild goose chase."

Mounting up, Vic rode past Joe and Darby without giving either of them a second glance.

The four men waded their horses into the muddy water of a fast-flowing stream and pushed through scrub oak and willow to the other side of the canyon. Here, the walls of Devil's Canyon sloped upward to meet vertical, barren cliffs and were made unstable by loose shale and rocks. If Malo Chavez's cave was here, shifting boulders might have covered the mouth or, worse yet, caused the whole ceiling to collapse. In such a case, the gold would remain lost to them forever.

Vic pointed down the canyon. "Shell, you see that big stand of cottonwoods? You and Darby start there and work your way back here. Keep your eyes open for anything that might be an opening to the cave. I don't care if it's just a crack. If you see anything at all, holler. Me and Joe'll start here and meet you halfway."

It occurred to Shell that all they had done today was backtrack. He and Darby headed down the canyon once again, left their horses at the edge of the trees to graze, and began to cast about for the cave's entrance.

They started their search without much enthusiasm, spending more time looking for sunbathing rattlesnakes than for the cave. Shell slowly climbed the rugged lower slope of the canyon wall, angling in a zigzag pattern over the rocks and testing the footing with each step. As he climbed higher, the wind reached him and played with his hair. He listened to it whistle through the trees. Pines and hardy little piñons clung tenaciously to the slope, as did Shell. It was steeper and higher than it had appeared from below, and he had to stop often to rest.

Panting, sweating, he hoisted himself onto a rock ledge and stood with his body doubled over and hands on his knees, struggling to catch his breath. From this point, he could see a distant mountain peak, possibly Wheeler, just visible over the opposite cliff. Its summit was still capped with snow. Below him in the canyon, the stream was a dirty ribbon.

"You see anything?" Darby yelled.

"No! Not yet!"

Shell sat down to tie his shoe, one leg dangling over the side of the ledge, and watched a lizard skitter out of sight at the boy's clumsy approach.

"This sun's sapping me dry," Darby complained, and he squatted in the shade of Shell's perch. "How can you stand not to wear a hat?"

"The hat bothers me more than the sun," Shell said shortly, still gazing down at the place where the lizard had been. There was a tiny beaten path, like the trail a pack rat might make, winding through the rocks and brush, and he followed it with his eyes to where it disappeared a few yards away beneath the same ledge on which he was sitting.

Drawing his shoelaces tight, he jumped down from the shelf and wandered aimlessly to the spot where he had lost sight of the pack rat trail. Here, the ground leveled off a little, and the ledge was higher than his head and dipped inward slightly so that he could stand beneath it. Part of the ledge had caved in, and the pack rat nest was wedged among the rubble. It was a huge, architectural conglomeration of sticks, trash, bleached bones, and cacti.

Shell remembered how he had once found a pocketknife in a nest like this. The blade had been chipped and rusty, but to a seven year old boy it was a real find. He had carried it around with him for months until his Aunt Myra got tired of looking at it and threw it away.

He kicked absently at the mound of trash, scattering it, and two gray shadows streaked away from their demolished house. Shell saw nothing of interest hidden among the debris and was about to turn away when he spotted a narrow crevice between the rocks. It had been covered up by the nest, and he knelt down to take a closer look.

"Hey, Darby, come here."

"See something?"

Shell raked dead brush and weeds out of the way. "I don't know," he said. "Let's find out."

They began removing the rocks, widening the crevice, and saw that it extended vertically between the face of the canyon wall and a heavy layer of rock that had fallen from above. Then Darby found the spur. It was a fancy one with the same large, sharp-pointed rowel Shell had seen Mexican vaqueros wear in California and in Mexico. Could this spur have belonged to one of Malo Chavez's men?

Excitement leaped within Shell, and he and Darby looked at each other and grinned. This could be it!

Darby drew his revolver and fired it into the air, drawing Vic's attention, then helped Shell lift the heavier rocks from the opening. Once these were cleared away, Shell was certain that this was Chavez's cave. The cavity angled inward, just like Vic had said, and before the ledge fell in, it would have probably been visible from the split rock down in the canyon bottom.

Darby put his weight against the slab of rock that half-covered the opening, dug in his heels, and pushed, but couldn't budge it. The cave's mouth measured about four feet up and down, but with the boulder in the way, it was only fourteen inches across at its widest point, a tight squeeze for any grown man.

Darby peered into the blackness of the cave. "Wish this rock wasn't here," he said. "Like it is, you can't see a thing."

"Vic's bringing some candles."

"What good's that?" Darby asked. "What we need are a few sticks of dynamite. Blow this big chunk of rock to kingdom come."

Shell nodded. "Yeah, and bury eight gold bricks under a ton of rocks just like it." He kicked at the boulder. "We need a pick and a single-jack, not fireworks."

"What's that about fireworks?"

At the sound of Vic's voice, both men turned to look at him. Joe was limping some distance behind.

"We may have found the cave," Shell told him.

He saw his partner's eyes brighten. Vic took in the situation at a glance, studied the terrain around the cave, and gave Shell a nod. "This is it," he said, and his heavy mustache lifted in a smile. "Nice work, boys."

CHAPTER SEVENTEEN

Gazing at the cave's mouth, Joe Finney lit his cigarette and cocked a hip to the side. "Too bad we ain't got a drill and a sledge," he commented. "I don't relish bustin' rocks, but if there's two hundred thousand dollars in gold in there, I wouldn't mind giving it a few good licks."

"Yeah, but who wants to go traipsing back to E'town to swipe somebody's mining tools?" Darby asked. "Not me."

"No need to," Vic said. "We've got Shell."

Feeling everyone's eyes on him, Shell looked up, caught Vic's meaning, and backed off, shaking his head.

"Come on, Shell," Vic coaxed. "You're about the right size."

"No way. Damn thing could be chock-full of rattlers for all we know."

Joe grinned, liking the prospect.

"If this was a den, you'd smell it," Vic said, and he began unpacking tallow candles, matches, and ropes from a stout leather satchel. "All I smell is rat piss. Now shuck that gunbelt so you won't get it hung up on the rocks."

"You mean you want me to go in now?"

"When did you think? Next week?"

Shell squatted in front of the narrow cleft and ran a hand over his face, rasping his palm against the black stubble on his jaw. He figured he could squeeze through all right, but it was what he might find once he was inside that worried him. He had a deep-seated fear of snakes. The thought of a whole den of them made the hair stand up on the back of his neck.

Joe lifted his hat and scratched his head. "I sure would like to be the first to see that gold," he mused. "I bet if I stripped off a few duds, I could make it in there as easy as Paxton could . . . since he's scared."

Darby laughed. "What about that beer belly you got hanging over your belt there?" he asked. "You get that wedged, and we'll have to look at your bare ass for a month till you lose some weight."

"Aw, shut up." Joe took a swing at him, but the boy dodged and laughed harder. Joe tried to ignore him. "What d'you say, Tex?" he asked. "Want me to do it?"

Chewing on a blade of grass, Shell raised his eyes to meet Joe's. "Be my guest."

"Hear that, Vic? He wants me to do it."

"He's not the one in charge here," Vic responded and thrust the candles and a spade toward Shell. "Get to it, kid."

Making no move to obey, Shell held the older man's gaze for a long, silent moment and had half a mind to refuse. But as usual, the notion was abandoned when he saw the first hint of anger enter Vic's eyes. He accepted the candles and grasped the spade by the handle, resting it across his shoulder.

"Malo said there was a short tunnel that led to the cave," Vic told him. "If that tunnel's not blocked and you make it through, you should find the gold buried shallow at the back of the cave. Each bar weighs around seventy-five pounds so you won't be able to carry them out by yourself through this narrow passage."

"Then how?"

Vic tossed him the satchel and one end of the rope. "Tie the rope to the shoulder strap. When you find the gold, put a bar in the bag, give the rope three good tugs, and I'll see if I can drag it out of the tunnel. You'll have to help it along whenever it gets snagged on something." He shrugged. "If that doesn't work, we'll think of another way. What's important right now is finding out if the gold is even there."

Shell lit a candle and poked it and his head into the cave entrance. The flickering glow bounced over the dusty rocks, and several daddy longleg spiders fled from the unexpected light. He could see only a few feet inside the passage. Beyond was blackness. Knocking ragged cobwebs loose above his head, he reached inside, wedged the candle between the rocks, and glanced over his shoulder at Vic.

"Anything else I should know before I go in?"

Vic stroked his mustache. "Just find the gold," he said.

It became obvious right away that Joe Finney wouldn't have stood a chance at entering the cave. Shell was several inches shorter than Joe and slim-built, yet it was all he could do just to squirm his way into the crack between the face of the bluff and the slab of stone. Once inside, it was no easier. Already narrow, the passageway that led to the actual cavern was cramped more by the rocks that had shifted when the ledge caved in. Shell held the candle as far out in front of him as he could, trying to see what lay ahead, but the light barely penetrated the terrible darkness.

Outside, he heard Joe tell Darby, "How much you want to bet it's a rattlesnake den?"

Careful not to blow out the candle with his breath, Shell pushed the spade out in front of him and inched forward, his body straining, twisting, squeezing between the sharp rocks at a painful cost. Slender or no, he was well-muscled through the shoulders, and in places he had to force his upper body between the walls of the passageway, shredding not only his shirt, but his skin, as well.

Bleeding from a dozen different cuts and abrasions, he paused to rest and looked back the way he had come. There was no daylight showing as he had expected, and he realized then that the passage was starting to curve.

Crouched sideways in the low, narrow tunnel, he tried to ease himself into a better position, dropped his candle, and was immediately engulfed in darkness. A sudden trapped feeling gripped him. This was even worse than the tiny jail cell in Lucky, Texas. He could actually feel the rock walls closing in on him, compressing his body, crushing the breath out of him. Strangling, he frantically struck a match and fumbled for the candle.

The light saved him.

Vic's voice, normally booming, sounded small and far away in his ears. "How's it going in there?"

Shell drew a long breath. "It's cramped as hell!" he yelled back.

"Watch for snakes!" Joe Finney this time. Distant laughter.

Shell spent a few more seconds glorying in the candle's feeble flame before he continued his slow advance. He hadn't struggled far when he came to a point where the passage widened enough that he could crawl on his hands and knees with little trouble. The floor of the passageway and the stone walls to either side of him were relatively smooth now and felt cool and clammy beneath his palms. The air had grown dank.

Groping behind the light of his candle, Shell almost fell headfirst into an abrupt drop-off. He drew back, lifting his candle at the same time, and discovered that the drop was a short one, less than five feet. He swung his legs over the side and jumped down.

His candle went out just as he hit the ground, and the black, silent emptiness was as shocking as if he had plunged into a pool of ice water. For the first time, he found he could stand upright and stretch his arms out to his sides without touching anything. The confining walls of the tunnel were gone. This must be the cavern.

Slipping the leather satchel from his shoulder, he struck another match and touched it to the candle's wick. The flame grew slowly, reaching for the smooth, concave ceiling, and out of the corner of one eye, Shell thought he saw something move. He whirled to face it.

A human skeleton met his gaze with bared teeth and vacuous sockets, and the flickering candle caused it to look as if it were twitching and jumping against the back wall of the cave where it was slumped. A few ragged shreds of clothing still clung to the bones, and cracked, leather boots encased feet that hadn't walked in years.

Startled, Shell backed off a step, tripping over something and bumping his head in the process. He glanced down. The floor was strewn with bones, many of them, perhaps all of them, human.

The initial shock gone, Shell massaged the growing lump on his head and looked around him. He noticed that strips had been cut from the dead man's boots, probably to be boiled and eaten by one of his comrades. Or by Malo Chavez before he acquired a taste for something softer than leather.

Shell picked up the satchel with the rope still attached to the strap and gave it a single hard tug to let Vic know he had made it into the cavern, then moved to the farthest wall where the gold was supposed to be buried.

He felt as if he had entered a tomb. The small chamber was roughly oval-shaped with a low ceiling, and someone had engraved a cross and the date 1867 into the smooth, stone wall.

Trying not to step on the many bones littering the cave floor, Shell chose a likely looking place to start digging, sunk the spade into the earth with his foot, and scooped up a shovelful of musty soil. Sounds of metal grating against gravel filled the small cave as he dug, and several times, he struck something solid but was disappointed when his gold turned out to be rocks. Having dug down about two feet and remembering the bullion was said to be buried shallow, he moved on, digging a little to the right of the first hole.

Shell continued in this manner until, much later, he came to the place where the skeleton was lying. If the gold was, in fact, buried against this back wall, it would have to be beneath the skeleton because he could go no farther.

His lungs laboring in the close air and his back aching, Shell rested a moment and eyed the skeleton with some misgivings. He didn't want to touch it, much less move it.

Maybe that was what Malo Chavez had had in mind, Shell thought. Bury the gold, drag a dead man on top of it, and hope that if anyone happened onto the cave by chance, they'd take one look at that skeleton and not want to tarry too long, never dreaming it might be sitting on close to a quarter of a million dollars in gold bullion.

He nudged one of the long, sprawled out limbs with his toe, then trying not to think about it, moved the whole stiff, flimsy framework of bones away from the wall. The skull disconnected and rolled off a short way from the body.

His candle almost burned out, Shell lit another, picked up his spade, and resumed digging.

Less than two feet down, the blade struck a hard, solid object that brought him to a jarring halt. Dropping to his knees, he cleared the stale dirt away with his hands, hurriedly now, his heart pounding, and felt the hard smoothness, saw the gleam in the candlelight.

"Jesus," he whispered, and sat back on his heels, eyes transfixed.

It was the yellow gleam of gold.

CHAPTER EIGHTEEN

Looking back, Shell supposed that deep down he had never really expected to find the Last Chance gold. He had thought about it a lot to be sure, had daydreamed about it, talked about it, and had dutifully stolen four stout pack mules on which the gold could be carried, but he had merely gone through the motions. Unlike Vic, he doubted the gold even existed.

This was one time that he was more than happy to be wrong. Moving the seventy-five pound ingots through the narrow tunnel and out of the cave proved to be the hardest job Shell had tackled yet, and the sun was on a downward dive when Vic finally dragged the last one outside. Smudged from head to toe in candle grease and clay, his muscles trembling with fatigue, Shell rested while the others lugged the bullion down the slope to the bottom of the canyon where Joe had picketed the horses and mules.

Though it was still daylight, the men pitched camp earlier than usual on a clear spot of ground at the edge of the cottonwoods. Darby roasted fresh venison on green sticks and baked biscuits in the ashes, while the others lounged around and relaxed. The bullion was stacked like cordwood in the center of camp, and the men were content to sit and stare at it.

Darby licked the grease from his fingers and smiled dreamily. "I've never seen anything so pretty."

"It's a sight for sore eyes all right," Joe agreed. Every so often, he would touch a bar, running his hand across the top of it, and wipe the dirt out of the grooved letters that had been stamped into its side. "I could look at it all day."

"Notice the color," Vic said. "Pale yellow. Shows it has a lot of silver in it."

Darby frowned. "You mean it's not pure?"

"No gold straight from the mill is pure."

Idly strumming Darby's guitar, Shell listened to their conversation and gazed at the bullion. He wished Joe wouldn't sit so close to it, as if he owned it. He watched him trace the inscription on one of the bars with a forefinger.

"What does it say?" he asked.

Joe glanced up at him. "What does what say?"

"The gold mark."

"Why, it's my name, of course," Joe said, and he grinned at them. "All eight bars have got my name on 'em."

Looking uncomfortable, Darby cleared his throat and favored Joe with a slight shake of his head.

Vic helped himself to another biscuit and leaned over to look at the inscription. "A.C.L.C.," he mumbled. "It stands for Adam Chaney's Last Chance."

Shell had forgotten all about Chaney. They had seen no more of him since that evening when they first rode into Devil's Canyon, and unlike other parties who dared to encroach on the crazy old man's territory, they had had no trouble from him.

Living the way they did, on the run most of the time, in hiding the rest, there rose a tendency to always be on the lookout for trouble. Yet Shell doubted their vigilance had anything to do with Adam Chaney's act of grace. He was simply waiting for them to find his gold. Now that they had it, he was sure to toss caution to the dogs and come after them.

Feeling generous, Vic broke out a bottle of brandy and passed it around by way of celebration. Lust for gold and a weakness for alcohol were all the four men shared in common, and it seemed a shame not to indulge a little.

Wanting to remain alert, Shell drank sparingly and noticed Vic and Darby did likewise. Even Joe Finney, who normally guzzled whiskey until his belly sloshed and his head swam, was uncommonly restrained tonight. But while he didn't drink enough to get soaked, it made him drowsy and loose-jointed, and Shell saw him nod off and jerk awake again more than once. No one wanted to sleep. No one wanted to take his eyes off the gold.

Vic, too, was watching Joe closely, and he nudged Shell in the side. "Sing us something. Something slow."

Not sure what Vic had in mind, Shell began to sing softly and watched as Joe's eyes grew heavier and heavier. At last, he could no longer fight off sleep and gave up. Lying on his back, he drifted off with his mouth open and one arm slung around the gold.

Darby was sprawled on his blankets a short distance away, and when he noticed Joe had fallen asleep, he sat bolt upright and turned an accusing eye on Vic and Shell.

"What's the big idea?" He rested a hand on his sidearm and kicked Joe awake. "Are you trying to sucker us into doing something stupid? Trying to get us drunk and off our guard?"

Shell quietly set aside his guitar.

Vic regarded Darby with an amused half-smile. "It almost worked, too," he commented and winked at Shell. "I'm giving you boys a taste of things to come. You'd better learn to sleep with one eye open and drink lots of coffee. I expect you'll be needing it before we reach Mexico."

Dragging a hand down his haggard face, Joe scowled. "What are you driving at?"

"Come on, boys. Surely I don't have to spell it out for you." Vic looked from one blank face to the other and shook his head in mock disbelief, that annoying half-smile still plastered on his broad face. He leaned forward. "The only thread that's held the four of us together this long is the gold. You needed me to find it, and I needed you fellas to help me find it. We used each other to reach a common goal. Now that the goal's been reached, where does that leave us?" His gaze fell on Joe. "Huh, Finney?"

"You're on a roll so far," Joe said. "Don't let me stop you."

Vic shrugged. "All right, here it is. If we stick together till we reach Mexico, we'd stand a better chance of making it there without getting robbed and killed." His smile widened. "On the other hand, it's likely we'd kill each other first."

Shell waited for Joe and Darby to say something. When they didn't, he broached a subject he knew none of them wanted to hear, one they had avoided talking about for too long.

"We could split up right now," he said. "If we did, the gold could still be divided equal between us. Two bars apiece. That'd be around fifty thousand dollars a man, fair and square."

No one said anything. Just as Shell had feared, they couldn't see past their own greed. Joe and Darby wanted it all for themselves and so did Vic. Shell wanted it all, too, but if his commonsense approach would prevent a killing, he was willing to settle with half the amount Vic had originally promised him.

Joe cast a sidelong look at Darby and finally spoke up. "We don't have to decide tonight. Let's think it over and talk about it tomorrow."

"Sounds good to me," Darby said.

They would bide their time.

CHAPTER NINETEEN

Suspicion and distrust oozed from the men's pores like sweat. Shell thought he could almost smell it. But the worst part was the doubt, the not knowing where he stood.

Not knowing if he could trust his own partner.

Throughout the night, he and Vic took turns keeping an eye on the gold, and Joe and Darby did likewise, but even when Shell's two-hour watches were over, he found it difficult to rest. Just as he would be on the verge of dozing off, some slight sound snapped him awake again.

Toward daybreak, however, exhaustion won out over vigilance, and it took Shell's usual early morning coughing spell to finally bring him around. He knew the minute he opened his eyes that Vic had allowed him to sleep through his last shift.

"You should've woke me up."

Both Vic and Darby were awake, and Joe was nowhere in sight. Vic had a pair of trousers spread across his lap and was busy patching a tear in the right knee.

"I wasn't sleepy," he said and ran his needle and thread through the coarse material.

"Just the same . . ."

Shell didn't finish. What difference did it make? Pouring himself some coffee, he sank back down on his blankets and warmed his hands on the hot tin cup. The sky was overcast with clouds and only now beginning to brighten with the dawn of a new day.

"That cough sounds a little less like it's gonna kill you every morning," Vic commented.

"It's not as bad as it was."

"About time."

"Yeah." He gestured at the gold with his cup. "Hard to believe, ain't it? Think we'll have any trouble selling it?"

Vic shook his head. "Remember old Johnny Leal? Down in Espia? He'll smelt it down and sell if for us for a small commission." Vic bit off the thread, thrust the needle into his hatband, and stiffly rose. Shell heard his knees crackle. "Then we'll divide the money and split up. Just like the old days, kid." Grunting, he tugged his pants on and gave Shell a gaptoothed grin. "Remember all that Wells Fargo gold Johnny smelted for us way back when? If we'd shown some sense and saved our money, we wouldn't be sleeping on the cold, hard ground and eating them chunks of lead that pass for biscuits."

"Hey!" Darby looked up. "My biscuits ain't heavy."

"No offense, boy," Vic said and turned back to Shell. "If I'd known I was gonna live this long, I would've done things different. I'd be a rich man today."

Shell nodded in agreement, and Vic fell silent.

What he had said rang true for them both. Before Shell got married, his money never stayed in his pockets for long. Spending money, he quickly discovered, was a hell of a lot more fun than saving it, and the minute you plunked a gold coin down, long lost friends crawled out of the woodwork and stuck to you like fleas on a dog. They lasted as long as the money flowed then drifted away in search of new prey.

Shell didn't mind. No one would ever accuse him of being stingy, and there was always more gold where that came from. Miners were digging it out of the mountains morning, noon, and night, and while the gold supply seemed endless, men's lives were not. Back then, Shell made it a point to enjoy today because tomorrow was a vague uncertainty.

It still was. But a wife, and later a baby, had made him see the importance of foresight, and his free and easy days were over. Even without the Last Chance gold, he and Sally had saved enough money to start over somewhere else. It would be easier this time.

A drop of rain splattered against Shell's cheek, and he glanced up at the low, gray clouds. Distant thunder rumbled.

Knowing it was about time he got up and watered his horse, Shell put if off a while longer and idly poked at their tiny fire with a stick. A burning piñon bough shifted on the coals and popped loudly, sending up a shower of yellow sparks, and Darby sprang to his feet as if he'd been stuck by a needle.

Both Shell and Vic looked up at him in surprise and watched as he let his half-drawn gun drop back into its holster. Vic had pulled his own gun in the same split-second as Darby. He eased the hammer down again but didn't bother to lower the muzzle. Not just yet.

The color slowly returned to Darby's face, and he turned on Shell with an angry scowl. "What'd you do that for?" he demanded. "You want to get killed?"

Shell regarded him coolly. "You're mighty damned touchy this morning."

"Yeah? I'll show you just how touchy I can be if you're not careful!"

"Is that a threat, Darby?"

There was an underlying edge to Shell's voice that hadn't been there a moment before, and he held himself still, keen eyes riveted on the boy's face.

In all these months of veiled threats and almost ceaseless badgering, he had lost his cool only once, but there had been a few instances when he had come very close, and this was one of those times. Darby James was smart enough to recognize the signs. He was also smart enough not to ignore them. There was too much at stake.

He averted his gaze, looking almost sheepish. "I didn't mean nothing," he mumbled.

"Glad to hear it." Shell tossed the dregs of his coffee into the fire, got to his feet, and slung his gunbelt around his hips. Buckling it on, he glanced toward the horses, then down at Vic. "If you see Finney before I do, tell him next time he takes it on himself to picket our horses, he might use a little more elbow grease when he drives those stakes down."

Vic looked up at him and frowned.

"I went to check on the horses once during the night and found your buckskin and my mare trailing their ropes up the canyon a short ways," Shell explained.

"Funny it was just ours that got loose." Vic sucked on his teeth and studied Darby. The boy refused to meet his gaze. "Sure makes you wonder."

"I know. Where'd Joe run off to anyway?"

Vic jerked a thumb in the direction of the cottonwoods. "Went to stand guard."

"How'd you pry him off the gold?"

Laughing, Vic shook his head. "I didn't have to. He left on his own."

Shell left, too, and walked out to where the horses and mules were picketed. Their heads jerked up at his approach, then recognizing him, they returned to their grazing. Only Snip continued to watch him. She nickered and walked toward him as far as her line would allow, stopped and waited, ears pricked forward, heavy forelock flopped over one eye. She had a roguish streak in her, and if it hadn't been for her love of sugar, he might have never caught her last night. Shell hoped the candy he had filched from Vic wouldn't be missed.

He fed the mare a lemon drop, untied her, and led her

across the meadow and down a narrow deer trail that wound through the willows to the stream. He talked softly to her all the while, saying whatever popped into his head, the words rolling out with an ease he didn't normally possess around people. Snip swiveled an ear in his direction, liking the sound of his voice.

The water was icy cold. Kneeling on the bank, Shell cupped his hands and drank, and a sharp pain shot up into his gums. He ran his tongue over his teeth, took another sip, and wiping his hands on his pants, stood up.

Instead of growing lighter, the sky was actually darkening. Shell glanced up at the heavy clouds in time to see a streak of lightning zigzag to the ground, flash, and disappear. Thunder crashed seconds later . . . and something else.

Shell's heart skipped a beat. He was almost certain he had heard a gunshot. Head turned a little to the side, ears straining, he waited for the thunder to roll across the sky and fade away. He listened intently. A dead silence hung over the canyon. Snip stood stock-still with nostrils flared and water dribbling from her mouth onto his already dew-soaked shoes.

An uneasiness in him, Shell clicked softly with his tongue and led the mare back into the trees where the shadows were deepest. He drew his revolver. One hundred yards of open ground lay between the willow thicket and camp, and while he wasn't about to risk crossing it now, he needed to be able to see something. He began to work his way to the edge of the thicket.

"Where you going, Tex?"

A man's shadowy figure slipped out of the trees in front of him and stood with his feet planted on either side of the deer trail. Shell drew up short, and the mare half-reared, knocking him off balance. It saved his life.

The hard blast of Joe Finney's Smith & Wesson rang in his

ears, and he hit the ground on his side, rolled over, and returned fire just as Snip pounded past him and crashed through the trees and brush. Another gunshot boomed like thunder. A bullet from a heavy caliber rifle spit dirt in Shell's face as he scrambled into the undergrowth, and he realized Joe wasn't the only one who wanted him dead.

Lying flat on his stomach in the wet grass, he waited and watched and quieted his breathing. Nothing stirred. His pulse thumped in his ears. He had been shot at before by men who favored the heavy, long-range buffalo guns, and the sound wasn't easily forgotten. Unless he was mistaken, that last shot came from a Big Fifty. Strangely, neither Joe nor Darby carried one. Vic didn't either.

So who did?

It was a moment before he heard the voices, two men speaking in hushed tones less than twenty feet away. Where he lay, the ground dipped slightly, and he didn't see Joe until he was almost on top of him. Their eyes met a split-second before Shell squeezed the trigger.

The shot was a hurried one at best, but it must have struck something of importance, for Joe yelped in pain and ducked back under cover. Shell didn't hang around to see what would happen next.

Slithering backwards on his stomach until he was hidden from Joe's view by thick brush and willows, he rose, crouched low, and ran as swiftly as the terrain would allow in the opposite direction. Behind him, Joe shouted, and four shots rang out in quick succession. The buffalo gun roared soon after, and Shell's feet flew.

He dodged his way through the tangled thicket, unmindful of the branches that snagged his clothing and slapped his face, and didn't stop until he stumbled onto a shallow wash. Giant cottonwoods had once stood tall through this area. Many of them were uprooted now and laying over, providing good cover, and it looked like as safe a place as any to make a stand. He might be able to hold the two men off him for at least a little while.

Straddling a rotten log, he slid down into the wash and sank to his knees. A thin rivulet of blood trickled from a scratch on his cheek. He swiped it away with the back of his hand, exulting in the fact that he hadn't been shot. It was a tight squeeze he was in, though, and he hadn't the faintest notion of how to get out of it.

Keeping a wary eye on his backtrail, he punched the spent cartridges from his gun and thumbed in fresh ones. He wished for a rifle. Handy as they were, six-shooters were for close work, and he wasn't so sure he wanted Joe and whoever he had with him to get that near.

He wasn't sure of anything right now. Where was Darby James? For that matter, where was Vic? Vic knew what to do in situations like this. He had tricks up his sleeve the devil himself couldn't have matched.

It never crossed Shell's mind that something might have happened to his partner. The possibility was inconceivable.

A light rain began to fall. The drops sounded like millions of tiny feet tapping the ground. Shell tucked his Colt inside his mackinaw to protect it from the rain and nervously ran his tongue over dry lips.

He saw them then, far apart and walking his way, Joe Finney and another man whom, from this distance at least, he did not recognize. He could see little of them through the trees, yet it was obvious they were looking for him. Despite the coolness of the morning, sweat broke out across Shell's face and mingled with the rain.

The man he didn't know suddenly drew up and motioned to Joe. He had cut Shell's sign. Their guns ready, they followed his trail more cautiously now, eyes scanning the trees for movement while water dribbled off the brims of their soggy hats. A flash of light and a snap, followed by a deafening clap of thunder, prompted the two men to duck down instinctively. They were almost within range. Shell eased the hammer back on his revolver and leveled the front sight on Joe Finney.

"Don't do it, Shell."

The voice came from behind. It was a low voice, barely audible above the rumble of thunder, yet it jarred him to the bone.

"Don't do it. I don't want to have to kill you."

It was Darby James. His face tensed, pale, Shell turned slowly to look at him. The boy was partly concealed by deadfall with only his head, shoulders, and rifle showing, and the rifle was aimed at Shell.

"Drop your gun," he said.

Shell cast a quick look at the two men out in front of him. They had spotted Darby and were running toward the wash. He didn't have a chance.

Lowering the hammer, he dropped his six-shooter in the mud.

Darby stood up. "Don't shoot! He's unarmed!"

Joe Finney was the first to reach them. He jumped down into the wash, mouth gaping, breath rasping, and yanked Shell to his feet by the back of his collar.

"Look what he did!" Holding onto Shell with one hand, he raised his arm up for Darby to see. Blood stained his shirt where a bullet had grazed his ribs and the inside of his arm. "Son of a bitch damn near killed me!"

"I told you we should've thought this through a little more."

"Yeah, and I told you to stay put and keep an eye on Taylor."

"Derned good thing I didn't," Darby replied and nodded at Shell. "He had you in his sights when I run up on him."

Joe swore and raised his gun. Shell saw the movement out of the corner of one eye and tried to dodge the blow but moved too late. The butt of Joe's Smith & Wesson struck solidly against his head, just above the temple. He felt the horrible impact, felt his knees weaken, the mud on his hands, on his face, cold mud giving beneath the weight of his body.

The last thing he remembered was an old man with dingy white whiskers peering into his face, and Joe's loud voice declaring:

"Tex, say howdy to my pa . . . Adam Chaney!"

CHAPTER TWENTY

Jesse was pretty put out with himself. Actually, it was Mother Nature whom he should have shaken his fist at, but that wouldn't have done him any good either.

He got caught two days ago in a downpour, and the rain had lasted just long enough to give him a bath and wipe out all sign of the tracks he'd been following. The soaking he hadn't minded, but to lose the trail meant he would lose more time, as well, something he had done plenty of already.

Lying wrapped in his blankets late at night, too tired to sleep after a day of mosquitoes, mud, and dead ends, Jesse wondered why he had ever decided to be a bounty hunter. Why couldn't he have chosen a safe, simple profession, something with a steady income and a degree of security? Thinking about it, he frowned and grunted in disgust. An undertaker wasn't exactly what he had in mind.

Jesse knew he lacked one all important requirement for a man in his line of work. Patience. Yet it was this very failing that drove him to find the shortcuts no one else would have thought of, to outthink his quarry—most of whom weren't too bright anyway—and know what they would likely do even before they knew it themselves.

Vic Taylor, however, was mighty slippery. Rarely did it take Jesse this long to bring in a wanted man, and it wasn't as if Taylor and his gang were lying low. They had kept the law on its toes all winter, making off with a number of Denver-bound gold shipments, and had literally gotten away with murder.

The killing of the Wells Fargo guard still puzzled him. Vic

Taylor had been known to crack a few skulls and smash some noses in his time, but murder, especially cold-blooded murder, had never been his style. After it happened, two top-notch detectives were dispatched from San Francisco with orders to track down and eliminate the renegades any way they saw fit. Hound dogs though these men were reported to be, they were also city slickers and unused to such a harsh climate, and their luck was worse than Jesse's.

All the luck seemed to have settled with Taylor and Paxton. Paxton in particular. Shortly after the Burkville-Dillon stage was hit, Jesse had questioned the three passengers and listened in disbelief as two of them openly praised Shell Paxton for his kind and generous nature—less than forty-eight hours after his partner blew a man's brains out. These people looked upon Paxton as a present-day Robin Hood, minus the stockings and feathered hat, which only served to complicate Jesse's task. Some actually went so far as to withhold information from him altogether.

Down here in the bottom of Devil's Canyon, however, uncooperative witnesses were no longer a problem.

The problem was finding the trail again. Familiarity with the countryside would have helped, but the descriptions he had received back in Elizabethtown were sketchy, for few men had ventured this deep into Devil's Canyon. At any rate, Jesse reasoned that the men he followed would stick to the most southerly route possible, bound for Mexico, just as Malo Chavez likely had done years ago.

The main canyon itself was said to extend for several miles in a roughly north to south direction where it then opened out into low, rolling hills and sagebrush flats. Beyond this was more of the Sangre de Cristo Range where the chain gradually swung to the west. Vic Taylor had a tendency to use open country as a means for putting the miles behind him, and once in the mountains, he invariably dropped out of sight. Jesse knew it would be in his best interest to catch Taylor and his men before they left Devil's Canyon. Positive they were southbound, he decided to stick with the main canyon and ignore the occasional side canyons that branched out from it. With a little luck and a lot of hard riding, he might overtake the outlaws before they hit open country.

It was on the third day after losing the trail that he heard the gunshots.

All night long the heavens had rumbled and growled, threatening to storm, and by morning the threat became reality. Jesse was saddling up when he saw a flash and glanced up in time to see lightning hit a tall pine on the canyon rim less than a quarter of a mile away. The tree went up in flames with a whoosh, and bits of it flew off into space, leaving behind only a smoking stump and a vague smell of charred wood and brimstone.

Spooked by the electrically charged air and exploding thunder, the dun gelding reared and tried to bolt, almost tearing the reins from Jesse's hands, and he was hard-pressed to calm the frightened horse. Swearing under his breath, he straightened the blanket and saddle, drew the girth tighter, and shrugged into his slicker.

He had just swung astride his mount when two gunshots cracked somewhere down canyon. He froze, head canted a little to the side as he listened to the echoes drum against the cliffs. Another shot rang out moments later, and a rare smile crossed Jesse's face.

He spurred the dun, striking off down the canyon at a fast clip, then slowed to a trot, warning himself not to let his eagerness exceed caution. There was no sense in getting caught in a crossfire. Better to let Taylor's gang fight it out among themselves first and even up the odds for him.

He rode with his revolver in his hand, sheltering it from the rain with his slicker, and cast an uneasy look at the angry clouds. Above him on the canyon's rim, trees swayed and tossed in the wind and rain. Finding a line of weakness in the canyon wall, he climbed to higher ground and struck a ledge wide enough for his horse to walk. So far he had been lucky that a flash flood hadn't washed him away, but one look at the rising stream told him not to chance it further.

Between claps of thunder, he heard more shots, and though it was difficult to judge distance by sound in such country as this, he doubted the shooters were far ahead of him. Had they found the Last Chance gold? Was that what they were fighting over? He thought of the lone horseman whose tracks he had seen and wondered if he was, in fact, Adam Chaney. He wondered how he tied in with Joe Finney.

Another bolt of lightning struck, very near, and he braced himself against the force of the storm as an occasional stray gust of wind tore at the fastenings on his slicker.

Sally Paxton learned the hard way that roughing it was not a pleasant experience. Bad weather, soggy camps, wet firewood—if it wasn't one problem, it was twenty.

Less than a half day's ride behind Jesse Watts, she had set out from Elizabethtown with high hopes, certain she would have no trouble keeping up with him. She followed the wagon road to the little ghost town of Last Chance, and the journey deteriorated from there on.

There was a ton's worth of difference between following a road and striking out into an unmarked wilderness, and despite the detailed map and directions given her by an old prospector in Elizabethtown, Sally lost her way twice en route to Devil's Canyon. Hopelessly turned around and lacking the skills required of any good woodsman, she searched vainly for a trail, a hoofprint, a landmark, anything that might help her find her way. She did finally come upon a trail left by two horses, but after following them for some time, she discovered an abandoned camp and recognized it as her own. She was wandering around in circles.

Ironically, it was the snowstorm that saved her. Cold, wet, and miserable, she stumbled onto a single set of fresh horse tracks the morning after the snowfall.

Sally had been trailing Jesse Watts ever since, pushing herself almost beyond her endurance in order to keep pace with him. It wasn't until a couple of nights ago, however, when she smelled the smoke from his campfire, that she realized how very near she was to him.

Now, crouched behind a rock outcrop, Sally listened to the fading gunfire and watched the man and horse take off down the canyon. In all these days, this marked the first time she had seen Jesse Watts. She had rounded a bend in the canyon, and there he stood, saddling his horse. Had it not been for the wind and thunder, she was sure he would have heard her.

She considered the danger of her position. Watts seemed to backtrack often, part of the reason, no doubt, that she had managed to overtake him, and the last consequence Sally wanted was to come unexpectedly face to face with this man. Yet to drop farther behind might mean losing him altogether.

Biting her lower lip, Sally stared after the horseman as he rode around a bend and out of sight. She decided to take her chances.

Thunder rocked the heavens, but Sally hardly noticed it as she carefully guided her horse around rain-slick slabs of rocks. She saw where deadfall had been cleared and knew Shell's party had passed through here.

Her thoughts never strayed far from her husband, and she

wondered now what he was doing. Had he been shot? Was he lying somewhere this minute, hurt and bleeding? Though he hadn't mentioned it, she had sensed the dislike between him and Joe Finney, but as always, it was Vic whom she feared the most. Unlike Shell, she was able to look at him objectively, and what she saw was a cold, ruthless man. A killer. Yet Shell's blind trust in him, as far as she knew, was unshaken. She could only pray that it didn't get him a bullet in the back.

Sally listened for more gunfire but was unable to hear anything over the wind and pelting rain. Perhaps, she reflected later, that was why she never heard the distant roar behind her until it was too late.

The canyon began to narrow, and rocks and boulders were many, the vegetation sparse. Sally crossed over to the other side of the stream where the bank appeared less broken, and holding onto her hat, she gazed up at the steep cliff. Hard drops of rain stung her face. She turned troubled eyes back to the stream. For some time now, she had been noticing a steady rise in the water level, and worry nagged at her nerves. Surely the canyon widened somewhere ahead, or if not that, perhaps she could climb to higher ground.

Lightning flashed in the darkened sky. Urging her mount to a canter, Sally scanned both walls of the canyon in search of a way out of the bottomland, but the cliffs, though broken, appeared unscaleable. The bay gelding she rode crabstepped a little and fought the bit, and Sally turned her attention to him, realizing he must have sensed her apprehension. Or was it something else? The packhorse, too, appeared nervous and was crowding close to her mount's hindquarters, eyes rolling, nostrils wide. Their fear was contagious.

Sally struggled to keep a tight rein on the bay, but once he got the bit between his teeth, she lost control. He stretched out, leaping rocks and logs and dragging the packhorse behind him, and though he ran only a short distance, it was to Sally an eternity before he answered her constant tug on the reins.

Her arms aching, she slowed him to a trot, then a walk, and drew rein. She was trembling almost as violently as her mount.

The rain had let up slightly, and a faint sound, like a muffled roar, reached Sally's ears. She twisted around in the saddle, listening, trying to separate it from the combined noise of wind and thunder and her own throbbing heartbeat. The sound was familiar. It reminded her of the nights she had lain awake in their little house in Texas and listened to the creek roar nearby after a hard rain. The roar of water . . .

Sally's face blanched.

She whipped the fidgety bay forward, glancing left and right as she fled, searching for a way out of the canyon, while behind her the roaring, rushing sound of run-off water from the mountains gradually swelled with power. To either side of her the canyon walls stood straight as soldiers. She wondered, could she climb to safety on foot, without the horses? The idea was instantly rejected. She must find a way out for them all.

Behind her for more than a mile, the canyon was inescapable and ahead of her lay uncertainty. She headed into the unknown. Her heart sank. Nowhere was there anything that looked like an outlet.

Then she saw it—a ledge, frightfully narrow and unstable, but a ledge just the same!

Swinging to the right, she rode across to it, dropped to the ground, and quickly knotted the packhorse's lead rope to the pommel of her saddle. Up canyon, the roar had increased in volume so that there was no mistaking its source. Sally seized the bay's reins and clambered onto the ledge.

At first the horses balked, then the bay suddenly lunged forward and up, scrambled for a foothold and stood trembling behind Sally while the packhorse followed his lead. Giving the reins a gentle tug, Sally moved on, stepping carefully, her right shoulder brushing the craggy face of the cliff. The ledge was barely wide enough for the horses, and rocks crumbled beneath their hooves. The packhorse slipped once, but the bay held firm, and they were soon moving again, steadily climbing.

They were only eight feet or so above the canyon floor when the path switched back in the other direction to a ledge still higher than the first. They followed it, gaining another twenty feet, and Sally glanced down. The stream was no longer a stream. Beaten to a froth, the water was roiling and muddy, and like some greedy monster, it was feeding off the rain rolling down from the mountains and growing stronger and stronger. Sally knew by the sound of that thunderous roar up canyon that it had yet to reach its peak.

Forty feet up, they drew to a halt. They could go no farther. Clutching the reins in one hand and digging the fingers of her other hand into a depression in the rock next to her, Sally gazed up at the cliff, dismayed. They weren't even halfway to the top, and though she saw a break where she might be able to climb to the rim of the canyon, there seemed to be no accessible route for the horses. They were practically balancing on the side of the cliff as it was, afraid to move, clinging to a pencil-mark ledge slick with rain and mud.

Earing her horse's head down, Sally reached around him for the saddlehorn and pried the knot in the lead rope loose. If one horse fell, at least he wouldn't drag the other one down with him. They were on their own now.

She managed to fumble her bedroll free of the saddle strings and pitched it and her rifle to a lip of rock above her head. Casting a wild look over her shoulder, Sally's heart almost stopped.

A wall of water was rolling down the canyon, crashing against the rock cliffs, tumbling uprooted trees and debris on its crest as if they were mere twigs. Sally saw at a glance that if she remained in her present location much longer, she too would be swept downstream!

Trying not to think of the fate of her horses, she dug her toe into a crack, grasped an angle of rock overhead, and pulled herself up to the bench where she had deposited her gear. She hugged the wall and shuffled sideways a few feet until she reached the vertical break in the cliff. Wind and rain lashed at her body, threatening to hurl her to the bottom of the canyon. She didn't dare look down.

Passing her arm through the sling of her rifle, Sally probed with fingers and toes for anything to help her gain more leverage and struggled upward along the broken fissure. Toward the top, the fissure narrowed and ended in a sheer precipice. She was balancing on her tiptoes, searching frantically for a way around it when the torrent struck.

Sally screamed as the wave crashed down on her. Her first sensation was that she was being pulled in every direction at once, that she would be torn apart by the terrible swirling force of the current. It tugged her feet out from under her, and muddy water filled her mouth, nose, and ears as she was submerged. Never had she felt so sure of her own death.

Arms and legs flailing, Sally fished for something solid to grab onto and fought to keep her head above water. She was carried downstream for several yards before the rushing current slammed her into the cliff. Though partially stunned by the impact, she reached out, clawing at the rocks and slick mud of the canyon wall as she was whisked past.

Her bleeding hands found possible salvation.

It was a rocky projection, a vertical column of sandstone jutting out from the cliff like a thumb. Choking, gasping, Sally wrapped her arms around it and clung there with the last of her strength. The roar of water filled her ears, filled her mind. She couldn't think. Paralyzed by fear and cold, she felt herself slipping . . .

A piece of driftwood butted hard against her shoulder, then glided past and careened down the canyon, and the sharp pain it left behind snapped Sally out of her daze. Throwing her head back, she sucked in a breath of air and looked up.

Her spirits lifted. Less than five feet above her head was a shallow pocket in the cliff where swirling flood waters had worn away the rock over the years. It was a small, open-mouthed cave. Sally wondered if she could reach it by climbing the sandstone pinnacle. She wondered if she had the strength.

Another wave splashed over her, engulfing her momentarily, and she gagged on brown water. Much more of this, and she knew she would drown.

Teeth gritted, arms and legs wrapped around the pinnacle, Sally used the eroded grooves in the sandstone to pull herself out of the water a few precious inches at a time, slowly squirming her way to the top. A blue vein stood out on her forehead. Her legs and arms felt numb. It was will alone that forced her tired muscles to work and strain, for by now there was nothing else left.

Once out of the powerful current, the ascent became easier, and she drew adjacent to the cave. She stuck a foot out, groping for a foothold on the side of the cliff. Her slick-soled boot slipped against the wet rock, then caught suddenly in a crevice, and grasping a sharp crag with her right hand, she used the last drop of will power she possessed to throw herself onto the floor of the cave.

Quaking violently, almost convulsively, Sally lay with her cheek pressed hard against the cold, wet stone, her hair splattered about her face in sodden strings. She gloried in the odd sensation of having something solid beneath her body. She felt as if she were still in the water, being tossed and tugged by the wild motions of the channel.

When she opened her eyes at last, she was facing downstream, and her gaze held on a pile of driftwood and trash that had snagged against the side of the cliff. It took her a minute to realize it wasn't driftwood. It was her packhorse. His lead rope had become tangled in the jagged rocks, and he was dead, his body broken and beaten and flung aside.

Sally choked back a sob and turned her face away.

She was uncertain how long she had lain there when something tickled the back of her neck. She struck it away, then looked up.

Midway between the cave and the canyon's rocky rim, a bony-faced man with deep-set eyes peered down at her and dangled a rope over her head.

"Grab hold!" he yelled. "I'll pull you up!"

It was Jesse Watts.

CHAPTER TWENTY-ONE

His eyes shut tight, Shell lifted his face to the rain and hummed softly to himself, unaware of the occasional annoyed look Vic threw in his direction. He was content for now to remain locked in his own little world. So long as he didn't move around too much or think too hard, the throbbing pain inside his head was almost bearable.

Out in the open, exposed to the wind and cold rain, he was sitting opposite Vic with his legs crossed Indian fashion and his hands tied behind his back. If he opened his eyes, he could look past Vic's left shoulder and see Joe and Adam Chaney. They had rigged a lean-to with pine boughs, grass, and two of the ground sheets, and while Joe busied himself sampling Vic's bottle of brandy, Chaney just sat and admired his long lost gold, gazing at it with half-closed eyes. He was a tall, narrow-shouldered old man with a roll of fat spilling over his belt and a long face partially hidden by a yellowed, unkempt beard. Joe favored him, and Shell thought if he and Vic had ever gotten a close look at the old man they would have known something was crooked.

As it was, the shocking revelation that Joe was actually Adam Chaney's son still hadn't quite sunk in.

Vic nudged him in the knee with his foot. "Hey. You all right?" His voice was low. "Say something."

Frowning, Shell opened one eye, then the other, and tried to focus on Vic. He was almost cross-eyed.

"I'm fine," he murmured and glanced over at Darby to make sure he hadn't heard. They had been warned not to talk to each other.

But Darby wasn't listening. He had been assigned to guard duty and was sitting huddled under his slicker a few feet away, staring toward the lean-to with a sulky scowl on his face.

Shell spoke to Vic but kept his gaze on the boy. "How'd they get you?"

"Joe and Darby held my attention, started talking about splitting the gold up . . . a bunch of nonsense." Vic grinned at him, blinking his eyes in the rain. "Next thing I know somebody's poking a gun in my back. I thought it was you at first, but it was Chaney. Darby got excited and fired off a shot without meaning to," he added and almost laughed. "Nearly blew old Chaney's head off."

Shell didn't say anything, didn't even crack a smile. Times like these, his sense of humor wasn't at its best.

"We'll get out of this," Vic said later, more serious now.

Shell met his gaze. "You bet we will. Soon."

The certainty in his voice surprised Vic. His hard, black eyes sharpened, asking the obvious question.

"All I need," Shell said quietly, "is the right time. Be ready."

Vic understood. "Can you handle it?"

"Just be ready."

Vic gave him a quick, searching look but didn't say anymore. It was just as well, for Shell had closed his eyes again and was humming another song, shutting him out.

For the past half hour, he had been working on the rawhide thong binding his wrists, gently twisting his hands, slipping them free a quarter inch at a time. The activity had given him something to think about besides what Chaney had in store for him. It had given him a glimmer of hope. His hands were small and supple, his patience infinite, and the combination of the three had eventually paid off.

179

Shell flexed and unflexed his hands, keeping them behind his back, and waited for an opportunity to use them.

The rain had stopped for the moment, and he looked toward the rushing stream. They were always careful where they made camp, which was a wise precaution, for the stream had flooded its banks several feet. Fortunately, the canyon was wide through here, and it wasn't likely the muddy, swirling waters would reach them.

Shell licked the rainwater from his upper lip, craving the moisture. The only dry part of him was his mouth. He watched Darby James stand up and amble toward them.

"You two look like a couple of drowned rats," he said, and hitching up his pants, he squatted next to them.

Shell's gaze lifted from the rifle resting across Darby's knees to the young, pimply face and wished the boy would straddle his horse and ride away and not come back.

Darby turned to him. "I warned you to get out," he said. "You should've listened."

"Maybe I should've."

"Want anything?"

Just your gun, Shell thought, but before he could figure out a way to grab it away from him without getting killed, he saw Joe and Adam duck out from under the lean-to and bog toward them through the wet grass and mud. Keeping an eye on Darby, he hastily looped the rawhide thong around his wrists, arranging it so, at a glance, it would appear that he was still tied. He drew a long breath and let it out, clearing his head, striving to relax.

Bottle in hand, Joe slung an arm around Darby's shoulders and took a swig. He looked from Vic to Shell. "How you feel, Tex? Head still hurt?" When Shell didn't answer, he kicked him in the ribs. "I'm gonna take pleasure in finishing you off, Paxton. Gonna take my time doing it, too.

Make sure you die slow."

Shell looked up at him, an intense hatred filling his eyes. Joe noticed it and sneered.

"Look at him. Doesn't say a word. Just stares at you like a damned Indian."

"I'd watch him," Adam Chaney remarked. "Them that say the least sometimes think the most."

Vic squinted up at the old man. "Well, Chaney," he said, "you finally got your gold. How does it feel to be rich?"

"Feels fine. Mighty fine." Chaney's washed-out eyes glinted. "To show how grateful I am to you for finding it for me, I ain't gonna kill you."

Vic looked interested. "Say, that's good news." He glanced at Shell, winked, and turned back to Chaney. "What's the plan?"

"I'm taking you boys back to E'town."

"You're turning us in, eh?"

"Yep."

Vic laughed. "You surprise me, Chaney. I didn't know you were so dedicated to law and order."

Scowling, Joe shook his head. "Hell, Pa, what do you want to go to all that trouble for? Let's shoot 'em and chuck 'em in the river. We don't need the reward money."

"It ain't the money I'm wanting," Chaney said. He puffed on his pipe a moment, then took it from his mouth and pointed it at Shell and Vic. "When I haul these two into town alive, you see if anybody talks down to me again. You see if they dare call me crazy."

Joe gazed at Shell, disappointed. "I got me a crow to pluck, Pa. Why don't you buy the town out and leave Paxton and Taylor to me. Then we'll both be happy."

Laughing, Darby said, "Now there's an idea. Maybe that's what I'll do with my share. Buy a town."

"Who said you were gettin' a share, boy?" Chaney asked.

Darby's grin dwindled. "Huh?"

"You heard me."

"But you said . . ." Darby turned to Joe, suddenly angry. "What's going on here? I did everything you told me to do. I deserve my share!"

Joe appeared vaguely surprised by his father's revelation but wasn't inclined to argue with him. He shrugged. "Guess that's the way the cookie crumbles, Darb."

Darby stared at his pal in disbelief, watched him tip the bottle up and swallow. His body trembled visibly. Vic and Shell exchanged glances.

Reaching in back of him, patting the ground, Shell's fingers closed on a rock about the size of his fist. He held on to it and waited.

"You can have the reward money," Adam decided.

Darby's face reddened. "It's not enough."

"Then you can do without. Makes me no difference either way."

"You promised me a third of the gold."

"I changed my mind."

Darby's grip on the rifle tightened. He slung it up and took a step forward. "Maybe this'll change it back."

A humorless smile twisted Chaney's lips. "You'll have to kill me," he said.

"I will if you don't give me my gold. I want it now."

"There's no way to divide it evenly. Not here. Not even if I wanted to."

"I want three gold bars," Darby said, "and one pack mule."

Adam Chaney eyed the boy with a flinty stare, knocked the tobacco from his pipe, and glanced at his son. "Joseph . . . take him."

Joe threw himself forward, springing into action like an attack dog let off its leash, but grabbed for Darby's rifle too late. The report echoed up and down the canyon. Shell heard the old man cry out when the slug ripped through him, saw him clutch his chest and stagger backwards.

Joe and Darby struggled for possession of the rifle, grunting, faces reddening, until suddenly Joe let go and swung the whiskey bottle at Darby's head. The boy ducked, barely avoiding the blow, but lost his grip on the gun, and it hit the ground.

It was the single break Shell had been waiting for. While Vic lunged to his feet and hurled his weight into Joe, Shell dove for the rifle. His hands had barely locked on the muddy stock when Darby slapped leather and yelled a warning. His voice was shrill, almost anguished, but there was no backing down in Shell now, and levering a round into the chamber, he fired a shot from the ground just as Darby leveled his Colt at him.

Six buttons down, a hole appeared in the boy's shirt, and his terrified screams tore at Shell's nerves.

Wild-eyed and cursing, Joe disentangled himself from Vic and palmed his revolver as Shell swung his rifle around. They fired simultaneously, the distance between them too short for a miss, and a slug slammed into Shell's left shoulder. All the strength drained from his arm. Joe dropped to his knees as dark, rich blood soaked into the fibers of his shirt but didn't go down, and he lifted his gun. Swiftly levering the Winchester, Shell braced it against his side and fired again with one hand. Joe Chaney gasped, coughed up pink froth, and slid forward onto his face.

In one violent, bloody flash it was over.

Swaying slightly, his left arm dangling limply at his side, Shell gazed down at Joe a moment, unable to believe the man was dead. He felt as if he were trapped in a dream . . . a night-mare. Nothing was real.

Darby James moaned, and holding his stomach, he rolled over onto his side, drew his knees up, and lay motionless on the wet ground. His ragged clothes fluttered in the wind. Farther away, Adam Chaney was sprawled in a mud puddle where he had collapsed after trying to crawl to his gold. One hand was stretched out, claw-like, seeking the bullion even as he died.

"Nice shooting," Vic remarked casually. "Didn't know you had it in you."

Feeling sick, Shell slipped the knife from Joe's belt and cut his partner's hands loose.

Vic worked the stiffness from his fingers. "Better stuff something in that hole in your shoulder 'fore you bleed to death," he said and moved past him to look at Darby.

Shell was a little shocked by all the blood. It seemed to be everywhere, spreading across the left side of his flannel shirt, dripping off the tips of his fingers. It was strange to him that the wound had only now begun to hurt. He didn't even remember getting shot. The bullet was still in him, probably lodged against a bone. Reaching inside his shirt, he held his wadded up bandana to the entry wound below his collarbone and watched Vic roll Darby over with his foot.

The boy was still alive, but for how much longer Shell didn't know. He'd never seen anyone who was gut-shot live for more than a day or two. His face was ghastly white and beaded with sweat, his eyes filled with misery and fear.

Shell knelt beside him.

"Looks like a free lunch for the coyotes," Vic said.

"He's not dead."

"No, but he will be."

"Don't rush him," Shell said quietly. Fighting off his own

weakness, he lifted Darby's shirt to look at the small, purple-rimmed hole above his belt buckle and frowned. It was all so senseless.

He started to rise when Darby grasped his arm.

"It's pretty bad, ain't it?" he whispered.

Shell looked down at him. " 'Fraid so, Darby. I'm sorry."

"Don't leave me here alone."

He nodded. "You rest easy. We're not going anywhere."

"Back when I was in the Army," Vic said, "traitors weren't granted any favors. They were executed."

"We're not in the Army."

"He'll slow us down. I've seen men in his condition linger for days."

Shell tried to make Darby more comfortable, and using the rifle to push himself up, he slowly rose and faced Vic.

"It's not likely he'll last long," he said, keeping his voice down. "Not without a doctor, at least. It won't hurt us to wait it out with him."

"Anybody'd think the two of you were best friends," Vic said irritably. "You care so damned much about him, why don't I leave you two here together, and you can enjoy each other's company all you want."

Shell's jaw tightened. He drew the blood-soaked bandana from his shoulder and gazed down at it. "Whatever makes you happy, Vic," he said at length. "Leave my share of the gold and a couple of pack mules, and you can be on your way."

Hands on his hips, Vic laughed and shook his head. "How do you expect to load and unload your gold with that shot up shoulder? Huh?"

Shell knew he was right. He had a knot on his head the size of a walnut, a .38 slug wedged inside his shoulder, and was so wobbly-legged he could hardly stand. It seemed strange to him that Vic, the biggest target among them, had escaped without a scratch. He had a crazy notion his partner was immune to bullets.

Vic reached out and rumpled Shell's wet hair like he would a child's. "You need me, kid. I reckon I'll stick by you."

Shell glanced down at Darby and was glad to see he was unconscious. "It's starting to rain again," he said. "We oughta get him under the lean-to."

"You go ahead. I'll take care of Darby. Then we'll have a look at that shoulder."

Shell studied him briefly, not understanding his sudden change of heart, but didn't question it. He turned, stepped around Joe Chaney's prone body, and left.

Slow, fat drops of rain splattered around him, unheard above the roaring flood waters and unnoticed by Shell. A black cloud floated back and forth across his vision as he wove his way to the lean-to, and each step sent a sharp, jarring pain through his shoulder. Shell crawled under the rough shelter and moaned softly as he sank down on Adam Chaney's smelly saddle blanket. He thought for a moment that he might have to vomit, but the feeling passed, and he lay still.

Something exploded, a loud, echoing crash, and the first thing that came to Shell's mind was that it had begun to thunder and lightning again. Then he wasn't sure. Raising up, he saw Vic standing over the boy with his gun in his hand, and the realization of what he had done washed over Shell like ice water.

Vic had, indeed, taken care of Darby James.

CHAPTER TWENTY-TWO

"You're a murderin' sumbitch," Shell slurred.

Vic finished wiping the blood from his knife and picked up the misshapen bullet he'd dug out of Shell's shoulder. He tossed it into the air several times, catching it in the palm of his hand, and glanced at his patient. "Are my ears playing tricks on me, or did you just call me a dirty name?" He dropped the bullet onto Shell's bare stomach. "Here's you a souvenir."

"You hear what I said, Vic?"

"I heard you. Now shut your mouth."

Shell rolled the bullet between his thumb and forefinger. It was still sticky with half-dried blood. Vic had had quite a time getting it out of him. He'd dug around, probed, and pried with his fingers and a pocketknife—the only surgical equipment available—for what seemed like forever. Biting his wrist to keep from crying out, Shell had begun to think he would rather keep the bullet inside him. He passed out finally, partly from the pain and loss of blood and partly from all the whiskey Vic kept pouring down him, and didn't come around until after his shoulder was cleaned and bandaged.

"Think you'll be strong enough to ride tomorrow?" Vic asked.

Shell tossed the slug into a puddle that had formed outside their shelter and watched the rings spread across the surface of the water.

"Hey." Vic kicked him on the bottom of the foot. "What's the problem? Cat got your tongue?"

Suddenly angry, Shell kicked back as hard as he could and

caught Vic square on the shinbone. The effort caused his head to pound, but he derived some satisfaction out of it anyway.

Vic laughed at him and rubbed his leg. "I'll take that as a yes," he said. "That's good news. We'll break camp bright and early tomorrow and be out of Devil's Canyon before dark."

Shell rolled his head to the side and felt the blanket damp beneath his right cheek. He looked at Vic. "You can go without me."

Sitting with his elbows on his knees, Vic chewed on a piece of dried meat and studied Shell with expressionless eyes. He didn't say anything. Just sat and chewed.

"You go on without me," Shell said again, thinking he hadn't heard him the first time.

"That's what you want?"

He nodded.

"You think that's a good idea . . . in your condition?"

"Better'n being around you," Shell said thickly.

Amused, Vic smiled and shook his head. "Whiskey draws the truth out, eh, Shell?" He sharpened a matchstick with his knife and began to pick his teeth. "All right, let's get something straight. What I did to Darby doesn't apply to you. If I wanted you dead and out of the way, I could have let you bleed to death an hour ago."

"Why didn't you?"

Vic appeared surprised. "Why would I want to?"

Shell could have given him eight golden reasons why he might like to kill him but opted to change the subject.

"You should've left Darby alone."

"What difference did it make? You'd put a dying horse or a dog out of its misery. Why not a man?"

"Nobody made you God."

His patience wearing thin, Vic leveled a stern look at him. "You're the one who shot him in the first place, and that's what's really eating you up."

"He was just a kid."

"His trigger finger worked as well as yours or mine."

"Darby wasn't all bad, though. He had some good in him."

"Shell, you're a naive damned fool. You know that?"

Shell didn't bother to answer. He wasn't sure what naive meant, but it was obvious to him it wasn't anything complimentary.

He watched Vic turn over onto his side and draw the leather bound Bible from his breast pocket. Flipping to a dog-eared page near the back of the book, he settled down to read. Shell thought it rather hypocritical of him, considering that he'd killed Darby James only a short while ago.

Vic peered over the top of the book at him. "Want me to read to you?"

"No."

"Suit yourself." He licked his finger and turned the page. "I guess I should have taught you how to read. Your pa would have wanted it." Lowering his Bible, he yawned and gazed outside at the dreary day. "I thought a lot of your pa. He was my messmate during the war, you know, and we stuck by each other through it all. That's the only reason I took you in when him and your ma died."

Vic fell silent and looked at Shell, studying him. "There was a time, Shell, when I'd have done anything for you. I loved you like you were my own son. Then you turned your back on me to marry that ornery girl and everything changed."

"I never turned my back on you," Shell murmured. "I just wanted a different life, that's all."

189

"Yeah, right when I needed you the most." Vic returned his attention to his Bible and sighed. "I'm getting old, Shell, and you were supposed to take care of me the way I took care of you when you were a youngster."

His words cut Shell like a blade. It was just as Sally had suspected all along. Vic was jealous! Jealous of his relationship with his wife and with his daughter when she had lived, and that jealousy had slowly evolved over time into resentment, and more recently, hatred.

It saddened Shell to think that the man he had considered all these years to be his father hated him, yet when it came down to making choices, he knew where his heart and his loyalty lay, and that was with Sally. No one, not even Vic Taylor, could lessen the love he felt for his wife.

Whiskey had a tendency to make Shell melancholy, and thoughts of his wife and daughter intensified the emotion. He had found himself missing Sally a lot lately anyway, mostly at night when it was quiet and nothing else was pressing on his mind, and his need for her was strong. Never had he known it was possible to care for someone so deeply.

"Vic, how come you never married?" he asked abruptly.

"Never saw any reason for it."

"You never met a woman you liked so much that you didn't want anybody else but her?"

Vic pretended to think about it, then shook his head. "Can't say I have. I like a variety. Why limit yourself to one woman?" He glanced over at Shell and grinned. "Hell, kid, you always did draw the women. They like you. You should take advantage of it."

"The kind of women you're talkin' about like anyone with pants on and a jingle in his pockets," Shell said morosely. "I'm talkin' about real women."

His choice of words gave Vic a good laugh. "What do you

think whores are?" he asked. "Fake women?"

Shell didn't give him the satisfaction of answering.

Tired and depressed, he slipped his .45 from its holster, and with his forefinger sticking through the trigger guard, he laid the pistol across his stomach. Now that Joe was dead, sleeping with a gun was an unnecessary precaution, but he did it anyway out of habit.

A slow, drizzling rain had begun to fall again. Shell drew the covers up around his chin, and his gaze centered on a leak in the thatch above him. He watched the drops stretch, stretch, break loose and fall, and counted each one as it struck the coffee pot with a tinny plink.

Fourteen drops later he was asleep.

A heavy fog descended into Devil's Canyon overnight, and when Shell awoke early the next morning it hadn't yet lifted. He lay still for a long moment, feeling an occasional fine spray of mist touch his face, and tried to gather his thoughts.

It had been a rough night. His blankets were tangled and twisted and wet with sweat, and his memory of the past several hours was a blur of strange, haunting dreams and interchanging extremes of hot and cold. Unbuttoning his shirt, he felt inside it to make sure his bandage hadn't slipped. The cloth was stiff, and the hair on his chest and under his arm was matted with dried blood. A burning thirst parched his throat, and he reached for his canteen.

Wincing, he propped himself up on one elbow, unscrewed the cap, and drank feverishly, gulping the water in huge swallows that hurt his throat. He drank until there was nothing left, flipped the empty canteen to the side, and lay back, exhausted. Only then did he realize he was alone.

He looked around him. Vic's rifle was propped outside the

lean-to, but his other gear was gone, and Vic was nowhere in sight.

Nor was the gold.

Holding his left arm against his side to keep from hurting his shoulder, Shell pushed himself into a sitting position and crawled outside. The fog was dense and rolling, and he saw only the horses and mules at first. Vic's buckskin was saddled. The mules were packed and ready to go.

A few seconds passed before Vic came into sight, striding up from the flooded stream with a dripping canteen in his hand. He looped the strap over the saddlehorn. Shell started to call out to him but changed his mind in the same instant. Instead, he watched with increasing apprehension as Vic moved toward the other three horses belonging to Joe, Darby, and Adam Chaney and stripped them of their halters. Vic whipped the horses across the rumps with a rope, and they galloped down the canyon and out of sight, the sound of their hoofbeats muffled in the wet grass.

Shell stared at Vic Taylor's broad back in disbelief. He meant to leave him here alone. He meant to take the gold and leave him here alone and afoot!

When Vic started to turn, Shell ducked back into the shelter. His gaze rested briefly on the man's Winchester rifle, and he wished he'd thought to bring it inside with him. Now it was too late. Vic would be coming back for it.

Shell patted his tangled blankets, feeling around for his gun, found it, and checked to make sure Vic hadn't unloaded it. An instinctive self-preservation blotted out everything else in his mind. Jaw knotted, eyes dark and stormy, he closed the Colt's loading gate, settled down within the shadows, and pulled the covers over him. He listened for his partner's approaching footsteps.

Moving silently, Vic appeared seconds later. He cast a

cautious look in Shell's direction, was satisfied that he was asleep, and bent to pick up his rifle.

"Where you going, Vic?"

The big man jumped as if he'd been struck by a snake. Shell raised up, unmindful of the pain that knifed through his shoulder, and leveled his gun at Vic. A nervous tic tugged at the side of his mouth.

"You wouldn't be fixing to skip out on me, would you?"

"It's not the way it looks," Vic said.

"Yeah? How is it then?"

Vic drew a slow, deep breath, squatted down, and rested his rifle on its butt so that it pointed skyward. "We've got trouble," he began. "I think I smelled woodsmoke yesterday afternoon, coming from up canyon. The way gold draws flies, it may be that somebody's on our backtrail, and that smoke couldn't have drifted far in this damp weather, so I figure they're pretty close. The quicker I get this gold to Mexico, the better." He looked Shell straight in the eye. "In the meantime, you stay put. I want you to keep whoever's following me off my back. Shoot their horses. Hell, shoot them. Do whatever you have to."

"Nice try, Vic."

"I'm not pulling your leg. There's somebody in this canyon besides us."

He looked serious, but Shell didn't believe him. "Yeah, three dead men," he said angrily. "Why don't you just admit it? You were gonna leave and not tell me a damned thing!"

"Well, you're partly right," Vic conceded. "I'm leaving without you. I want you to stay here, rest up, and when you get your strength back, you can join me in Espia."

Shell leaned forward. "It'd take me quite a spell to get there, considering I'd have to walk."

"Walk?"

"I saw you run the horses off."

Vic stared at him, half-amused, half-irritated, not trying very hard to hide his indifference to the matter. "Not much gets past you, does it?" he asked and shrugged his shoulders. "Good as you are with horses, I expect you can catch one up easy enough. That bay gelding of Darby's is gentle as a lamb." He gestured at Shell's wounded shoulder. "You won't be able to sling a saddle on him for a few days, though."

"And that'll give you a good head start, won't it?"

"Look here, Shell, I'm leaving you with a job to do. Somebody's trailing us. I want you to stop them." Vic winked and flashed him a reassuring smile. "You may not be up to a long, hard ride, but I know you can still pull a trigger."

"Cut the crap, Vic. Darby was right all along. You can't be trusted. You mean to keep the gold for yourself. Always did."

Vic shook his head. "That fever's messing up your thinking."

"Oh, my thinking's real clear." A crooked little smile turned up the corners of Shell's mouth, a smile that didn't touch his eyes. "Clearer than it's been in years," he said and cocked his .45. "You've given the orders long enough. Now it's my turn."

"I told you a long time ago to never point a gun at a man unless you're fully prepared to use it. You're not." Vic slowly extended his left hand, palm turned up. "Fork it over."

Shaking his head, Shell changed his position so that he was kneeling on one knee. "I want you to put that rifle down, give me your gunbelt, and then back off. I'm taking your buckskin and my share of the gold. You can catch up your own damned horse."

"And what if I decide to keep my guns and ride out of here like I planned?" Vic asked in a low voice. "What would you do about it, Shell? Shoot me?"

"I wouldn't have no other choice."

Vic's face hardened. "You spineless little bastard," he muttered and regarded him with contempt. "You've never had the guts to stand up to anyone in your whole sorry life."

He rose abruptly and left.

"Vic!" Shell scrambled after him, staggered to his feet, and stood with his legs apart to keep from falling. His face was bloodless. "Vic, don't make me shoot you in the back!"

Halfway to his horse, Vic stopped but didn't turn to face him. Shell watched him, tensed and waiting.

"If I remember right," Vic said quietly, "I gave you that six-shooter for your seventeenth birthday." He half-turned in order to look over his shoulder at Shell and eased his rifle up so that it was slanted across his chest. "I'd hate to think you'd actually use it on me."

Shell started to speak, but before he could get the words out, Vic swung around, and he knew the parley was over.

The instant the big man moved, Shell crouched low and shot from the hip. He felt the Colt jump in his hand, smelled the gunsmoke. Vic fired wild as he stumbled back a step, and Shell squeezed off another round. A red streak appeared across the side of Vic's head, and his body went slack, buckled, and slumped to the ground in a boneless heap.

His thumb curled over the hammer of his gun, Shell approached the fallen man and looked down on him with haunted eyes. Vic lay sprawled on his back, arms and legs spread wide, mouth gaping.

There was a bullet hole in his slicker, directly over his heart.

Shell holstered his gun, sidestepped Vic's body, and moved toward the big buckskin gelding on unsteady legs. Grasping the saddlehorn, he rested his forehead against the animal's warm shoulder and closed his eyes a minute while the world swirled around him.

The dizzy spell passed, and he stepped into the saddle. The stirrups were too long for him, but he was so unstrung he never noticed. Sick at heart, he walked his horse down the canyon, leading four heavily laden pack mules behind him, and slowly faded into the fog.

CHAPTER TWENTY-THREE

Jesse had planned to ride off bright and early the next morning following the storm and leave Sally Paxton on her own, but found he couldn't bring himself to do it. Though he wasn't chivalrous in nature, leaving a woman alone in this wild country with no horse and nothing to defend herself with wasn't something he wanted on his conscience. He had seen men hang for less than that. So instead of leaving, he lingered over his morning coffee and watched her sleep, admitting to himself that it was rather nice having a woman's company. That she had said less than two words to him and hated his guts was beside the fact.

It was hard to believe that this petite young woman had followed him all the way from Elizabethtown without his knowledge. Accustomed to being the hunter and not the hunted, Jesse hadn't given his backtrail as much attention as he should have. Sally Paxton seemed to possess a surprising amount of grit and determination, considering she had traveled this far without getting lost or killed. Yesterday's brush with death could have happened to even the most seasoned outdoorsman.

Anxious to hit the trail, Jesse rose finally and nudged her in the side with his foot. Her eyes flared open.

"Let's go."

She raised up on her elbows and flipped back the covers.

"Your boots never dried out," he said and handed them to her.

She took them without looking at him or saying a word, and he walked to his horse. Below him in the canyon, the fog

197

blocked his view of the bottoms. He decided it would be best to ride along the canyon rim until the visibility improved.

Seeing that Sally was ready to go, Jesse swung into the saddle and looked down at her. Her face was scratched and bruised, and she was favoring her right leg.

"I guess you'd better ride behind me," he said.

"I'll walk."

"You'll get left behind. I figure to catch up with your husband today. That is if he's still alive."

She met his gaze with hostile eyes. "You won't catch him."

"Don't think so, uh?"

"No, I don't. He's the better man."

"You'd be surprised at the number of people who seem to agree with you," Jesse said irritably. "But you'll never know if I catch him or not if you lag behind. Better come along with me."

She didn't have much choice. He helped her mount up, and as soon as she was settled, he touched his spurs to the dun and headed south. It amused him that rather than hold onto him, Sally clung instead to the saddle strings in order to keep her seat.

He turned his head to the side. "Don't try reaching for my gun or knife, or I'll leave you for the wolves."

"Wolves don't attack people." She sounded scornful.

"No, ma'am," he said, "but they do eat dead people."

She didn't have anything to say to that.

If the dun minded the extra burden, he wasn't showing it. Jesse was glad he'd taken the trouble to ship him down from Denver instead of buying one of those plugs at the livery stable. His gait wasn't smooth, but he could be trusted to get you wherever you were going.

They hadn't ridden far when three shots, one right after the other, sounded ahead of them in the canyon. Jesse drew rein.

"Sounds like somebody's doing a little target practice," he said, and spotting a game trail leading down into the canyon, he took it.

The water in the stream had already receded several feet, and the grass was laid flat from the rushing current of the day before. When the sun edged its way over the canyon's eastern rim, steam rose from the wet earth.

Jesse rode up on the three dead men unexpectedly, the ground being low where they were lying, and he immediately shucked his rifle. In the clearing beyond, he spotted the lean-to and saw that it was empty. Sally's chin bumped his shoulder as she looked around him at the bodies.

Scanning the area for any movement and glancing at the nearest cliff to the right of him, Jesse dismounted and stole cautiously toward the dead men with Sally clipping his heels.

Two of the bodies were lying close together. One was Joe Finney, shot twice through the chest, and the second was the James boy. The third man Jesse didn't recognize but suspected he was the same lone rider whose tracks he had seen earlier.

Darby James had been shot once in the stomach and once between the eyes. Jesse knelt beside him, waved a swarm of flies from the boy's face, and briefly examined the gunshot wound in his forehead. He recognized it as a direct contact wound, where gases from the gun muzzle had expanded between bone and skin and ripped a ragged, star-shaped pattern into the skin surrounding the bullet hole. It had been a cold-blooded murder, something Vic Taylor was capable of.

The bodies of all three men showed signs of having been dead since yesterday.

"Must've been quite a shoot-out," Jesse mused and slipped his knife out of its sheath. "Finney and James are worth about three hundred dollars apiece, last I heard. Better turn your head. You may not want to see this."

Having given her fair warning, Jesse ran the knife's sharp blade around Joe Finney's hairline, cutting through to the skull, then took hold of his hair and peeled off his entire scalp. He took the boy's next, damaged though it was by the gunshot, and with the two scalps grasped in his left hand, he rose and glanced over at the woman. She looked sick.

"Once rigor mortis sets in, you can't do much else," he explained.

Tethering his horse, he motioned for her to follow him and moved on, sticking to the cover of the trees as much as he could and trying to watch both in front of him and behind and still look for sign. Rain had washed away the tracks from the previous day, which would make it easier to find the fresh ones from this morning.

He approached the lean-to by a roundabout way and squatted at the edge of the cottonwoods. Birds twittered in the bushes, and above him in the treetops, new pale-green leaves slapped together, stirred by a light breeze. There was saddle gear scattered about the campsite, but no horses and no men.

Sally smiled and brushed a long strand of hair from her face, tucking it behind her ear. "Looks like you missed them," she said.

Her elation wasn't lost on Jesse. It would be in his best interest, he knew, to tie and gag her, and he guessed he'd do it before he set out again after Taylor and Paxton. She was feisty, though, and he dreaded the struggle.

He moved out of the trees. While he doubted anyone was around, he remained watchful in crossing the clearing to the lean-to. Rifle up and ready to shoot, he peered inside the empty shelter. Something lying in the entrance caught his attention, and he stooped and picked it up.

Sally drew up beside him. She took the bloodstained shirt from his hands and examined it in silence.

"Your husband's?"

She nodded, face downcast, and absently picked at the frayed edges of the bullet hole. Jesse thought she might cry, but when she looked up her eyes were dry.

"Shell's been shot before. Twice," she murmured, as if the fact was suddenly important to her.

Dew still clung to the grass except where the outlaws had passed back and forth, leaving tell-tale paths that were easy for Jesse to follow. He followed one particular trail to a point midway between the lean-to and the trees and discovered a spot of ground where the grass was pressed flat, as if someone had lain down. Squatting on his heels, he found a small amount of blood smeared on a blade of grass and decided it was more likely that someone had fallen down. He began to circle the area, spiraling outward from the flattened grass, and picked up an empty cartridge shell and a small, black book.

Jesse turned the book over in his hands, surprised to find that it was a Bible. The outside front cover was badly scarred where it had deflected a bullet. Opening the book, he saw Vic Taylor's name scrawled in black ink on the front page.

He showed it to Sally.

"It's Vic's all right," she said. "He always carried it in his breast pocket, only it was in better shape the time I saw it."

"Looks like it may have saved his life," Jesse remarked.

It also looked as if Shell Paxton and Vic Taylor had put an abrupt and violent end to their partnership. This then accounted for the three gunshots they had heard earlier.

Jesse found a single footprint and recognized it as Paxton's. While searching for more tracks, he saw where the young outlaw had mounted his horse and led the mules away.

201

The pack animals' hooves had sunk deeply into the mud. They were evidently carrying a heavy load, and Jesse had a good idea as to what it was. Taking the gold and leaving his partner for dead was not characteristic of Shell Paxton, but Jesse had seen men do worse than that where the yellow rock was concerned.

So what had happened to Vic Taylor? Where was he?

It was Sally who stumbled onto Taylor's tracks below the canyon's western wall, not far from the abandoned camp. Jesse followed the man's footprints, noting his irregular, staggering gait. On the rocky slope, trailing him became more difficult. Jesse scouted around and found a trace of mud on a rock slab higher up the slope where Taylor's foot had slipped. Though only a thin skim of mud, Jesse noticed it had not yet dried despite the sun shining upon it.

Suddenly uneasy, he lifted his hat, wiped the sweat off his forehead, and squinted up at the high cliff. It was possible the outlaw had seen or heard them ride up minutes ago and was attempting to scale the cliff to safety. There were numerous nooks and crannies up there, and like a wounded old grizzly bear, Vic Taylor could be holed up in any one of them and watching him this very minute.

Grasping Sally by the arm, Jesse moved back into the cover of the trees. The woman had to trot in order to match his long strides.

"Did you see Vic?" she asked.

Without answering, he dragged her to the ground and forced her to sit at the base of a slim cottonwood.

"Damn you! What do you think . . ."

Jesse clamped a hand over her mouth. He felt her teeth scraping against his palm and hastily whipped off his bandana and gagged her before she managed to bite him. Eyes wide with anger and fear, she struggled and kicked until he lost patience and slapped her across the face. His hand left a red signature on her cheek.

"Sit still," he hissed.

She stared at him with sullen eyes, reminding him of the way she had looked the first time he ever saw her, almost a year ago. Some things never changed.

There was a rope on one of the discarded saddles, and cutting it down to size with his knife, Jesse gripped her wrists so hard she didn't dare try to pull away and tied her hands together on the other side of the tree trunk.

"I'm going after Taylor," he told her. "I won't be long."

He walked to the edge of the trees again and was studying the lay of the land, mapping out the best cover, when movement high on the cliff across from him caught his eye. He dropped to one knee. Vic Taylor appeared briefly on a narrow ledge a hundred feet or more above the canyon floor, half in shadows, half out, and the rifle in his hand winked at Jesse when the sun touched the barrel.

Lips pressed tightly together, Jesse rested the Winchester's butt against his shoulder, but the outlaw dropped from sight behind a sandstone buttress before he could draw a bead on him. Moments later, he spotted Taylor again, lower and farther to the right of where he had seen him last. The man was slowly working his way down from the cliff, and at the same time, moving up the canyon. It didn't take Jesse long to figure out what it meant.

The cagey devil was doubling back for Jesse's horse!

CHAPTER TWENTY-FOUR

Shell went over the killing of Vic again and again in his mind but could think of no way in which he could have avoided it. Vic had dealt him a severe blow, had tried to doublecross him, and it all happened too fast for thought. Shell had had no choice in the matter. Or had he? He didn't know. Nothing made sense to him anymore.

He stopped a short way from the old campsite to make coffee and simply sit and think. He wasn't sure what to do next. As in the years before he married and settled down, he depended on Vic more than ever, always looking to him for the answers, trusting his judgment. Life without Vic Taylor to make all his decisions for him was going to take some getting used to.

Glancing over at the mules, Shell thought about the gold. It was hard to believe that it was his and that he was rich. A lot of money had passed in and out of his pockets over the years but never two hundred thousand dollars, and the sight of those heavy packs should have lifted his spirits. Strangely, it failed to stir him.

He rose after a while, doused the fire, and walked to the stream. Once he had washed his face in the cold water, he felt better, more like himself. Remembering he hadn't reloaded his gun, he did so now and gazed back the way he had come. It was time he returned and gave Vic a proper burial.

Folding his wet bandana, Shell tied it around his head and adjusted the stirrups on Vic's saddle before mounting. The buckskin was so tall he felt as if he were riding a camel. He still had hopes of finding Snip again and whistled for her several times on the way back to camp, thinking to draw her attention. Given the black mare's flighty nature, there was no telling how far she had run yesterday.

Ducking a low-hanging branch, Shell broke through the trees into the clearing and drew rein. His breath caught in his throat, almost choking him, as he gazed down at the spot where Vic had fallen.

The body was gone!

Cold fear washed over him. He palmed his gun, stepped down from the saddle, and tethered his horse and the mules. Common sense assured him a man with a slug in his heart couldn't possibly get up and walk away. His eyes, however, told him a different story. Vic wasn't here.

He knelt where the grass had been pressed down by Vic's weight. This was the place all right. He found a little dried blood on the grass, and Vic's Bible lay off to the side. Thinking it must have slipped out of Vic's pocket when he fell, Shell picked it up, and his fingers touched the gash in the leather cover. He glanced down at it, saw where the bullet had struck it, and immediately looked around him, searching the trees.

So Vic was alive. He let the Bible slip from his fingers and faded back into the shadows.

You should have been more cautious, he told himself. You should have made sure he was dead.

It seemed to Shell that the nightmare would never end, that it would go on and on until he finally got killed. His luck couldn't last forever.

He led his horse and the mules deeper into the trees, scanning the ground for Vic's tracks. He had half a mind to leave, just ride away and forget him but realized it was a foolhardy notion. Vic would catch up with him sooner or later. It might take months, it might take years even, but he would find him and kill him and enjoy every second of it. Vic never left a score unsettled.

A movement off to his left startled Shell, and he stopped in his tracks. He whirled to face it, gun raised, and couldn't believe his eyes.

She was sitting with her back against a cottonwood trunk, gagged, hands tied, tangled, auburn hair falling over her shoulders and brushing the ground. A streamer of sunlight slanted across Sally's face when she turned to look at him.

Shell's first impulse was to run to her, but caution interceded. Partly screened by scrub oak, he waited, searching for a trap. There didn't seem to be anyone else around.

"Is it safe?"

His voice was barely above a whisper, but Sally heard him and answered with a quick nod of her head. She stared at him with large eyes as he emerged silently from the underbrush, crossed the few feet of open ground that separated them, and dropped down beside her.

Touching a finger to his lips, he slipped the gag from her mouth and drew his knife.

"Shell, I thought you were dead," she gasped. "We couldn't find you, and I . . . ."

"Shhh." He severed the rope binding her wrists with a single upward thrust of his knife, and she clung to him like a frightened little girl. He held her close for a moment, then lifted her to her feet and led her back to where he had left the animals.

Once hidden behind the scrub oak thicket, Shell took a quick look around him before turning his attention to Sally.

"Now, who's we?" he whispered. "Who brought you here?"

"It's Jesse Watts, Shell. He's been following you for days. I tried to warn you but . . . ." Her voice faltered, and she shook her head.

He gripped her shoulders. "Jesse Watts is here?"

"Yes."

Searching her eyes, her face, Shell touched the bruises on her forehead and right cheek, and a swift anger leaped through him like a flame. "He did this to you?"

She shook her head. "No. He didn't do anything. It's a long story, Shell, and not enough time to tell it. We have to get out of here."

"Where is he?"

She didn't say anything, as if hesitant to tell him.

"Sally, answer me. Where is he? Did he go after Vic?"

She nodded finally and pointed out the direction Watts had taken.

"How long has he been gone?"

"Not long."

"Stay with my horse," he told her. "If I'm not back for you pretty soon, leave. Take the mules with you."

"You really found the gold then?"

"Yeah, and it's liable to be the death of us all," Shell replied.

Unbuckling his cartridge belt, he handed it and his .45 to Sally and stepped toward the buckskin. Vic kept his old sawed-off shotgun looped to the saddlehorn by a leather strap, and Shell lifted it free and stuffed a couple of handfuls of shells into his jacket pocket.

"How's your shoulder?" Sally asked. "Is it very bad?"

Shaking his head, he broke the shotgun open and checked that both barrels were loaded. "If you meet up with Vic or Watts, either one," he said, "run like hell and shoot to kill if you have to. Understand?"

She stared at him. "You mean, Vic . . ."

"Just do like I say, Sally."

He turned away, but she caught him by the sleeve.

"I could go with you," she whispered.

"No. You stay here."

He kissed her on the lips, squeezed her hand, and left.

It didn't take him long to pick up both Vic's and the bounty hunter's sign. He followed the tracks slowly at first, then quickened his pace once he had familiarized himself with both sets of footprints and was fairly certain where they were leading him. Exactly what he intended to do if he caught up with the two men wasn't yet clear in his mind, but one thing was certain: He wouldn't spend the rest of his life looking over his shoulder, wondering when one or the other of them would show up on his doorstep. No matter the outcome, it must end here. Today.

Sally's presence worried him more than anything. If something happened to him, she would be left to fend for herself. Shell suspected Watts had intended to use her to get at him, and anyone who would drag a woman into this rough country for that purpose couldn't be expected to care what happened to her once his goal was achieved.

Shell suddenly remembered what Vic had told him, about having smelled woodsmoke the previous afternoon. It hadn't been a lie, after all.

The trees began to thin out, and Shell grew more cautious, stopping every few feet to look and listen and seeking cover wherever he could along the way. As he neared the canyon wall, the land grew steeper and rockier, the tracks less distinct. Higher up the slope, the trail disappeared altogether.

Gray-faced and weak, he stopped to rest on the shady side of a boulder and dug the heel of his left foot into the gravel to keep from sliding downhill. The air smelled of rain-fresh earth, sage, and piñon. It smelled like summer. It felt like summer, too, though it wasn't. Shell wiped a drop of sweat from the end of his nose and rubbed his palm on his jeans. He heard the distant braying of one of the mules in the canyon bottom.

Surrounded by tumbled boulders and brush, his field of vision was greatly restricted. Vic or Watts either one might be hiding practically under his nose, as unaware of his presence as he was of theirs.

Wounded and afoot, Vic must have lit out the instant he spotted Jesse Watts and headed for this rocky terrain where his trail would be hard to find and there was good cover. But what then? Shell wondered, What would you do in Vic's place? Run? Hide? No, that didn't sound like Vic. Vic would take the initiative so that he came out on top.

He'd make a beeline for Jesse Watts' horse.

The idea occurred to Shell suddenly when he remembered he hadn't seen the bounty hunter's mount when he found Sally. Watts must have left the horse farther up the canyon.

Rising stiffly, he began working his way in that direction, winding through the huge dull-beige boulders and scratchy brush, careful not to slip on the loose shale. It was rough going, and his head throbbed painfully, keeping tempo with the rapid beat of his heart, yet he dared not leave the shelter of the rocks, not for a little while at least. He threw his head back to study the cliff often, half-expecting to see either Vic or Watts aiming a gun at him, but they never showed, and he continued on, ducking low, stubby-barrelled shotgun gripped in his left hand.

He had reached the shade of a barn-sized block of granite when he lost his footing and fell to his hands and knees. Gravel and fragments of rock showered to the bottom of the slope and plates of shale clinked together like broken pieces of pottery.

"Taylor!"

Shell froze, scarcely daring to breathe.

"Taylor, I know you're up there. Come on down with your hands in the air!"

Partly sheltered by the granite block, Shell didn't move. The bounty hunter was somewhere below him. Hearing Shell when he fell but unable to see him, Watts had mistaken him for Vic.

A rifle shot cracked the stillness. The bullet caromed off a boulder to the right of him and whined off into space.

Crouched down in the shade with his shoulder butted against the cool granite, Shell swore under his breath and looked around him. The granite block was half-buried in the face of the slope, a slanting upheaval of rock with a rift scribbled down the middle of it, and the top appeared fairly flat. Shell eased out of his cramped position. Digging his toes into the wet, gravelly soil, he climbed higher, edging alongside the length of the granite block until he drew level with the top of it. He pushed his shotgun out in front of him and hoisted himself onto the smooth surface.

Another shot ricocheted off the rocks, but Shell paid it no mind. Rainwater had collected in a depression next to him, and he drank deeply of it and brushed the back of his hand across his mouth. Protected on all sides by talus and jumbled boulders and below by solid granite, he lay flat on his stomach, nosed his shotgun over the edge, and peered down between the V-shaped cleft at the piñons near the bottom of the slope. If that was where Watts was hiding, he envied him the shade but not the mosquitoes.

He saw a flash of blue—the color of Jesse Watts' shirt—as the man darted out of the piñons and ducked behind an outcropping of rock, moving closer. Shell cocked the right barrel of the shotgun and waited for him to try that again.

Perhaps a minute later, the brim of Watts' battered black hat and the barrel of his rifle appeared around the right side of the outcropping. Shell looked down the short barrels of his gun at him, planning to give him a taste of buckshot, when the unexpected happened.

Preparing to make a dash for another point of cover, Jesse Watts had leaned forward slightly, and the gunshot caught him in mid-dive. It seemed to come out of nowhere, an echoing crash that caught Shell so unprepared he almost dropped his scattergun. Watts landed hard on his stomach, and his rifle skidded out in front of him, clattering against the rocks. Shell saw him make a desperate grab for the gun in his waistband when five more shots blasted away at him, near misses that sent chips of rock and grit flying into his face. A sixth shot struck his revolver just as he lifted it to return fire, and he immediately froze, lying on his side, hatless, gaze fixed on something above and to the left of Shell.

"All right, all right!" He lifted his hands, one of them bleeding, and nodded toward his fallen rifle and broken six-shooter. "I'm unarmed now. Don't shoot!"

Wriggling around on his stomach, Shell looked between a crack in the rocks next to him. Vic had risen and moved out into the open and was now standing on a narrow ledge a few feet up the side of the cliff with his rifle aimed at the downed man.

Shell was close enough to him that he could see the blood blackened and crusted around his ear and down his face and neck. The big man swayed a little, dangerously close to the edge.

Shell couldn't believe his good fortune. Had Watts not heard him and thought he was Vic, he might have continued up the canyon, and Vic would surely have seen him and killed him. As far as he knew, neither man was aware of his presence.

"You must be Jesse Watts, the famous manhunter," Vic

said, his voice thick with sarcasm.

"That's my name. How'd you know?"

"Seen your ugly mug in a newspaper once."

Watts raised his bleeding hand higher. "You're quite a shot."

"I generally hit what I aim at," Vic conceded.

"So why didn't you kill me?"

Vic grinned at him. "Are you in a hurry, Watts?"

The bounty hunter hesitated, not saying anything, not daring to move, and Shell thought he looked scared. He didn't blame him. Jesse Watts was a hard man, but he wasn't as dangerous as Vic. Shell knew Vic intended to kill the man, saw the murder in his eyes, heard it in his voice, and it repulsed him.

Vic regarded the man below him curiously. "Watts, you disappoint me. A fella with your reputation . . ." He shook his head, still smiling. "I expected more out of you than this. Of course, anyone who'd let a piss ant like Shell Paxton get the better of him couldn't amount to too much."

Watts shrugged. "Looks like he bested both of us."

"Not me, he didn't. I've been a step ahead of him all along."

"Really? Tell me about it," Watts said, playing for time.

"Well, let's just say he's got a hell of a surprise in store for him when he breaks into those packs."

Shell listened to the words, feeling his anger mounting, surging through his veins, hot and ugly. He fought to control it, to bury it inside him.

Drawing a deep breath, he raised up on one elbow. "Hey, Vic! Why don't you let me in on the secret now? Spare me the suspense."

His voice was calm, almost friendly, like a man asking the time of day, but its effect on the two men was as great as if he'd shouted at the top of his lungs. Vic wasn't smiling anymore.

Shell pushed himself to his feet and slung his shotgun up. He brought it to bear on his former partner. The rising wind whipped around him, ruffling his hair, blowing his jacket open, and he felt the blood wet and warm against his skin where his wound had broken.

Gazing up at Vic on the ledge, he lifted his foot and hooked his heel on the sharp-edged rock in front of him, steadying himself. "How about it, Vic? What's the big surprise?"

"Well, what d'you know," Vic said thinly. "Speaking of the piss ant, here he is."

Shell let that slide. "I asked you a question."

The initial shock fading somewhat, Vic appeared more at ease and in control. He cast a casual glance at Shell, noted the shotgun in his hands, and grunted. "If you'd taken the time to look into the packs on them mules, you might not be so eager to blow a hole in me."

"What are you talking about?"

"The gold's not there."

Shell's eyes narrowed slightly. "You're a liar. The packs . . ."

"The packs are filled with worthless rocks," Vic replied, and he laughed softly, enjoying himself at Shell's expense. "Looks like the joke's on you. Remember me telling you I thought somebody was on our backtrail?"

"Yeah. So?"

"So yesterday evening while you were asleep, I hid the bullion just to be on the safe side. This morning, I loaded the mules with rocks to make it look like they were packing the gold." He glanced at Shell again and winked. "You're welcome to try to find it."

Shell stared at him, unable to believe he had been so easily duped. "You're lying," he repeated, though not with much conviction.

"Why would I lie?" Vic nestled the rifle's butt more comfortably against his shoulder. "Our friend, Mr. Watts, thought he could get the reward money and the gold, too. Instead, he'll just get a chunk of lead."

The bounty hunter was still lying on his side in the hot sun, thin, sweaty hair plastered to his skull, neck crooked back, gazing up at them with squinted eyes. He didn't look so tough anymore.

Vic started to sight down the barrel at him.

"Damn it, Vic, no!" Shell thumbed back the shotgun's second hammer. "Put the rifle down!"

"You'd take his side over mine?" Vic demanded, and he shot an angry look in Shell's direction. "You kill me, you'll never find the gold. The rain last night wiped out every trace of sign. Think about it! Do you want the gold or not?"

"I want you to put the gun down," Shell said. He stood ready, alert to every move of the man on the ledge less than forty feet away from him. "I'm not gonna stand by and watch you kill another unarmed man. It's over."

Vic let the rifle slip down a little from his shoulder, and for a moment, Shell thought he would listen to him. He never got a chance to find out for sure.

A strong gust of wind whistled through the brush, whirling around them, and the force of it threw Vic off balance. Already unsteady on his feet, he took a faltering step to the side, and Shell yelled a warning as a weak spot in the ledge crumbled beneath the big man's weight.

Pebbles and fragments of rock crashed down from the cliff face, and Vic fought uselessly to regain his footing. He pitched forward, arms flailing, clawing at empty air, and Shell watched in horror as he struck the boulders below, flipped over, and tumbled helplessly down the slope, faster and faster, until his body finally lodged against the rocks and brush near the bottom.

His face set and grave, Shell jumped down from the granite block and carefully descended the rugged slope, angling toward Vic Taylor's motionless body.

The bounty hunter had risen to his feet, but he made no move to pick up his rifle, and looking past him, Shell saw the reason why. Following the sounds of gunfire, Sally had located them and was now holding her gun on the bounty hunter. Sweating and out of breath, she watched as Shell struggled down the slope to Vic Taylor.

Vic was lying on his face in the mud. Panting, Shell rolled him over with his foot, almost hesitant to look at him, and dropped down on one knee. Vic stared blindly at the blue sky, his pupils dilated, not responding to the bright midday sun shining full in his face. Blood trickled from his mouth, nose, and ears. Sure that he was dead but remembering the last time he'd been sure, Shell passed a hand over the man's open mouth, then felt for a pulse. Nothing.

Closing Vic's eyes, he gazed down at him a long moment, at this man he had once respected and trusted, and tried to sort out his feelings. He couldn't. He was numb. Perhaps tomorrow or a week from now he would feel something, but today his emotions were as dead as the man who lay before him.

"No one could survive a header like that!" Watts shouted. Ignoring him, Shell rested a few minutes before climbing back up the slope. Halfway up, he looked at Sally. Their gazes met, and he saw the answer in her eyes even before he asked the question.

"The gold's gone, isn't it?"

She nodded. "It's not on the mules. I'm sorry, Shell."

He looked around him, looked at the high cliffs on either side of the canyon. Those towering, rocky cliffs. There were a million and one places where Vic could have hidden the gold. A man might search for years and never find the right one. Shell didn't even know where to start.

The whole sorry situation struck Shell as funny. He ran a hand through his hair, laughed, and glanced over his shoulder at Sally.

"Pretty good, huh? Even dead, Vic still has the upper hand."

He turned and climbed the rest of the way up the slope to his wife and the bounty hunter and stopped a few feet from Watts. He studied the man, the dislike evident on his face.

"Since when did you start hiding behind a woman's skirts?" he asked.

Watts scowled. "Is that what she told you?"

"No. I'm asking you."

"Your wife followed me here of her own free will."

Shell looked at Sally, waited for her to deny it. She didn't say anything. He wasn't surprised. It sounded like the sort of daredevil stunt Sally might pull, tagging after Jesse Watts without a thought as to the trouble she might run into along the way. It was a wonder she hadn't been killed, yet he found himself smiling at his young wife in admiration.

"Sally," he said, "you're something else, you know it?"

She frowned at him, tensed up, uncertain. "You're not mad?"

"How could I be?"

Lowering her gun, Sally smiled back at him, a smile of pride in herself and sheer happiness at being at her husband's side again, and bobbed the barrel of her gun at the bounty hunter.

"So what do we do with him?"

Beady eyes shifting from Sally to Shell, Jesse Watts dug papers and a sack of tobacco from his shirt pocket and rolled a cigarette with shaky fingers. Shell watched him, the shotgun in his left hand, pointed down.

Jesse squirmed under his intent stare. "Want a smoke?" he asked brusquely.

"No thanks."

Nodding, Jesse returned the tobacco to his pocket and gazed down at the dried blood on his hand where Vic's bullet had nicked him. "Looks like I owe you one."

"For what? It's not like I pushed him over the edge."

"He was fixing to kill me. You tried to stop him."

"I'd have done the same thing for a dog," Shell said, his voice flat, direct.

Jesse looked him in the eye. "I believe you." He drew on his cigarette, cheeks sucking inward, and exhaled slowly. "Even so, I feel I owe you something, and I don't like to be in debt." He dropped his cigarette and ground it into the mud with his boot.

Shell wasn't expecting any favors from this man or anyone else, but before he could say as much, Watts bent over, picked up his hat, and gestured with it at Vic.

"I'll be needing a pack animal. I don't guess you'd sell me a mule, would you?"

Shell thought about it, taking his time, and finally shrugged. "I lifted around seven hundred dollars off you in Lucky," he said. "Take the mule, and we'll call it a fair trade."

"Damned expensive mule," Jesse remarked.

"Take it or leave it."

"I don't guess I'm in any position to argue, am I?"

"Nope. We'll leave you one mule tied at the camp down canyon."

Jesse nodded and glanced up at the sun. "I'm obliged. In

the meantime, I'll get my horse and see if I can find an easier way down to Taylor's body so I can load him up before he gets too stiff to handle." He looked at Shell then, settling his hat back on his head, tugging the flat brim down low over his eyes. "Then I guess I'll be on my way."

"I guess you will," Shell agreed. "All the way back to E'town where you'll let everybody know that I'm dead and buried."

"Dead and buried, eh?" The faintest of smiles flitted across Jesse's face. "Guess that means you'd better not be robbing any more trains," he said. "We can't have the law thinking I'm a liar."

Shell watched Jesse Watts pick up his rifle and walk away, half-expecting him to suddenly wheel around and fire a shot at him and was prepared for it, but the bounty hunter never broke his stride. He never even looked back.

Sally drew up beside Shell, leading the buckskin, and hooked a finger beneath one of his belt loops.

"You're letting him go?" she asked.

"Yeah." He looked down at her, at her bruised, sunburned face, and gently brushed the tips of his fingers across her cheek. "I'm letting him go. He's letting me go." He smiled a little and took the reins from her hand.

"We'd better get our gear and animals together and make tracks out of here before I change my mind."

They were about to leave when a sudden movement in the heavy brush startled them. Shell whirled to face this new and unexpected danger, one hand gripping his gun, the other protectively grasping his young wife's shoulder as he pushed her behind him. He stared in disbelief as a velvety, white-tipped nose materialized through the brush, followed by a pair of delicate ears and a sleek neck. Dark, mischievous eyes gazed at the couple through a black mane tangled with burrs.

Laughing, Sally slipped from Shell's side and walked out to greet his estranged horse. Snip nibbled playfully at her outstretched fingers, soft lips popping, nostrils quivering. It was a good sign, Shell decided. His two favorite girls were with him again.